Holiday Hearts

HEARTS OF HIDDEN HILLS

SUSAN LOWER

TIME GLIDER BOOKS

Holiday Hearts Copyright © 2023 by Susan Lower. All Rights Reserved.

All rights reserved. No part of this book may be reproduced in any form or by any electronic or mechanical means including information storage and retrieval systems, without permission in writing from the author. The only exception is by a reviewer, who may quote short excerpts in a review.

Cover designed by Fantasia Frog Designs

This book is a work of fiction. Names, characters, places, and incidents either are products of the author's imagination or are used fictitiously. Any resemblance to actual persons, living or dead, events, or locales is entirely coincidental.

Susan Lower
www.SusanLower.com
ISBN: 978-1-945274-11-4

Printed in the United States of America

First Printing December 2023
Time Glider Books

Remember not the former things, nor consider the things of old. Behold, I am doing a new thing; now it springs forth, do you not perceive it? I will make a way in the wilderness and rivers in the desert.

Isaiah 43:18-19

Holiday Hearts

Chapter One

You'll come home for Christmas.

It had been a demand more than a request. One Caroline Adams would have never dreamed of not obeying. Not when it came to her mother, or her entire family, for that matter. But on the whole drive back from Louisville, her stomach sank, and she felt the onset of the flu.

Because deep down, she knew her life would never be the same. She had to go home. There was nowhere else for her to go. And here she stood, opening the door of her little two-door sedan outside of her aunt's bed and breakfast. Grateful for Aunt Marge's offer of a place to stay for her and Duke, Caroline had offered to lend a hand—especially over the holidays.

Her father never allowed animals inside the house. As she reached behind her to clip a leash on Duke's collar, she couldn't bring herself to put him out in the winter. "What a perfect gentleman you are." She scratched behind one of the Golden Retriever's ears.

Shamelessly, Duke, and not to mention and her sister, had been the main reasons she refused to move back in with her parents. Besides, she didn't need to hear any more "I told you so's." *Not today. Not ever again.* She tucked a strand of hair behind her ear, closed the trunk of her car, and hefted her suitcase in her arms. Everything else could wait.

She hadn't noticed the blue pickup truck. Did Aunt Marge have a guest? It would delight her aunt as she didn't get many and most came during the holidays. Like Caroline, people booked rooms when family didn't have enough space for their visit.

Aunt Marge would have whisked the cobwebs from the house and prepped a room just for her. The one with tiny pink rosebud wallpaper and her great-grandmother's vintage vanity in the corner, which had been hers until she took off for college.

Right before the door, she remembered to tap the snow from her boots. Duke scratched his front paw against her leg. She'd take him out later. Right now, she wanted to get inside to let Aunt Marge know they'd arrived. With no need to knock, she turned the knob and pushed the door open. "Aunt Marge?"

When no answer came, Caroline frowned. She slipped her feet from her fur-lined boots. In the next room, she heard a clunk before a thud and a slew of words she couldn't make out.

"Auntie Mar?" She entered the hall off the kitchen with Duke at her side.

Aunt Marge preferred to keep this old place after Uncle Ivan passed and both her sons took off to join the Army. Scott came home at times, but Nevin never would. His loss was still fresh in her aunt's heart, as if it had happened yesterday instead of almost a decade ago.

Aunt Marge didn't seem to be around, but something had fallen, and someone had spoken. Curiosity got the best of her. She slid open the pocket doors to the dining room, expecting to see another dog or even one of the ladies from church.

"Well, if it isn't Samuel Brink." Her old classmate from high school stood on a chair and balanced a chandelier in his hand.

Duke growled softly. Caroline laid her hand atop his head to reassure him she didn't need protection. But by the look on Sam's face, he hadn't been expecting anyone to walk in.

"Caroline." He resembled one of those circus performers

standing on a tightrope and trying to keep his balance while holding a pole. Only it wasn't a pole in his hands, and he wasn't juggling balls, either. He held on to Aunt Marge's crystal chandelier. The tip of his ears turned red, and his eyes grew wide, more like a kid caught with his hand in the candy jar, rather than a circus performer.

She did her best to hide her amusement, stifling the giggles threatening to erupt from inside her.

"Do you need some help?" she managed, in her calmest voice, the one she'd taught herself to use before letting her mind jump to conclusions. Surely, Samuel Brink had enough money in his pockets and shouldn't need to swipe Aunt Marge's crystal chandelier. That, and there were so many other things a lot easier to pick up and take off with inside the house than to pull utilities from the ceiling—pretty and expensive as they might seem.

Sam turned and looked down at her from over his shoulder. "Nah. I got this."

"Mind if I ask what you're doing?" She leaned back against the doorjamb. Sticking her hands in her coat pockets, she realized she hadn't thought to take it off when she came inside.

His back stiffened as he turned to the chandelier. Perhaps he had a problem with her watching him. Maybe he didn't get many girls in her position, standing to admire his backside. But then again, Sam had always been the shy one in their class. Those dark, unruly locks of hair from his youth no longer hung to his nose.

How many years had it been since she last saw him? Six? Maybe seven?

There had been a lot of them that year who had left and gone to different colleges. Not that it was unheard of, but there hadn't been many in their class to begin with. Luke Meyers had gone off to play college baseball and got picked up by the minor leagues. Not everyone in a small town could find success.

Caroline glanced over to check on Duke, sitting and panting at her side. She looked back at Sam. He'd changed since she remembered him last. He'd aged, filled out all those lanky boy limbs, and toned up to become a handsome man. Not that she was looking at him, but she couldn't help noticing.

He pulled a screwdriver from his back pocket, and while holding the chandelier in place with one hand, tightened the screws.

Dropping Duke's leash, she motioned for the dog to stay as she walked around the large oak dining table to where she could stand on the other side and see Sam's face. "Are you sure you don't need any help?"

"I got this. There was a short in the wire, making the lights blink. I asked Marge if she was sure she wanted me to fix this, but she said Halloween was over and she didn't need any rumors of a haunted bed-and-breakfast going around."

Caroline laughed. It sounded just like Aunt Marge to say and think such a thing. "So, you're an electrician?"

He grinned at her, the dimple of his youth still there. "I'd heard you were coming back to town."

What felt like the calming of the seas in her stomach churned again. "I suppose Aunt Marge would have told you." What did it matter? This was Sam. The boy she sat in the back seat on the bus with throughout elementary and middle school years. His family lived in the small white house down the road from her family's farm. His dad worked for the pig farmer between their place and hers.

And never once had Sam looked at her as he did now. Stepping down from the oak dining chair, his grin split wide open, and her heart did not just do a flutter. But it did.

"Actually"—he tossed the screwdriver into a toolbox on the table she hadn't noticed before— "it was your sister."

Aunt Marge would have his hide if his toolbox scratched her polished, gleaming wooden tabletop. Caroline folded her arms in front of her. "Janelle."

It had to be Janelle. Her other sister, Brenda, didn't keep track of other people's lives. Janelle, on the other hand, worked at the bank with Luke's older sister Lisa, who'd left town when Caroline was fifteen and married to the Shaw boy. Lisa came home less than a year later, one baby in hand and pregnant with another. Caroline remembered the scandalous gossip about Lisa leaving her husband. It spilled over in calls from her sister. At the time, Caroline wasn't sure who needed her prayers more, Lisa or the ones spreading the gossip.

Janelle knew everyone and everything around town. One reason Caroline moved to escape the politics of living in a close-knit community.

And the isolation that came with it.

"Then I suppose she told you my entire life story as well?" Caroline didn't want to do this right now. She shouldn't talk to him. They hadn't spoken in years. When they'd gotten to high school, she'd stopped sitting in the back row on the bus. The other guys in their class made her feel unwelcome, and Sam did nothing to stop them.

Sam closed his toolbox, his voice softened when he said, "She figured you might need a friend. Seeing how we might have a few things in common."

"You can't believe everything my sister tells you."

Sam grabbed his toolbox, and before he left, offered her these words. "I'm here if you ever want to talk."

Chapter Two

Talk? He couldn't believe he just said that. Out loud. What kind of moron would she take him for? He couldn't have gotten out of there fast enough. He'd tried not to stare at her. For all he knew, he'd crossed the wires on Marge Thompson's chandelier and the lights would explode the next time she flicked the switch instead of blinking on and off like a haunted house.

Never one for words, Sam searched for the wedding band on her finger before she'd crossed her arms and hidden her hands from him. Janelle would have been right about her sister's current relationship status. Wouldn't she?

He had to get going. He promised Bryson he would be there when his little guy got off the bus from school in a few hours.

If he were looking to date since coming back home to Hidden Hills, Caroline probably would have come to the top of his list. They'd been friends once when they were kids. At first, it was because they both got on the bus before the others, Caroline, then him. They stole the back seats away from the other kids. It made him feel important. Sitting on the other side of the row of seats from her made him feel like they'd taken the role of king and queen of the back seats. Even now, it made him want to laugh.

Tall, curvy, hazel-eyed beauty. And her waves of chocolate silk hair... Caroline Adams was far from a child, but for the sake of his bubbling-up emotions, he'd try to keep her there. He promised her sister he'd be her friend, someone the same age she could talk with and hang with in this small blip of a town. And certainly, he'd keep his promise. She'd come home but wouldn't stay. No one ever stayed here for long. No one but him, except for a few others like Luke Meyers, with no other choice because of family obligation.

Sam had been the first, though. It seemed right. Coming home had been a blessing for him and his son.

"Welcome home, Caroline," he said, starting up the engine of his truck and pulling away from Marge's place. He needed to get back to work. There would be time later to catch up with Caroline. For now, he'd give her some space. Knowing her family, she'd get very little of that once they discovered she arrived. He'd wait out the holiday, and by then, he'd know if she would stay. Knowing her family, he couldn't blame her for coming to Marge's first. The Adams family could, at times, be overwhelming to anyone. Like his family, they all meant well, and he prayed for Caroline to find comfort rather than anxiety from all the attention soon to come her way.

No one ever said coming back to Hidden Hills had been easy. Big dreams, expectations, and a city tempting to give them everything. A small part of him hoped Caroline would find what she needed right here, where they all grew up.

He owed it to Bryson, more than himself, to wait before opening his heart to any idea of letting someone else in again. According to Janelle, Caroline's life took a turn and forced her to leave the city. She'd given him more details that weren't any of his business. If Caroline wanted others to know why she left, she'd tell them when the time suited her. Everyone had a right to their privacy.

Sam had his own reasons for leaving Louisville. He went to college and fell in love with a pretty girl who seduced him with promises and dreams but left him with Bryson. His son. The baby he brought home from the hospital was birthed by a woman who would have given him up for adoption. He'd offered to marry her, should have done that in the first place. She'd have nothing of him and his proposal. Wanted nothing of the life he envisioned for them.

With no way of knowing her faithfulness in their relationship, he claimed Bryson. His son and Megan's, but before he even got the baby out of the car from the hospital, she was off to find her next high.

He pulled up beside the barn. He closed his eyes for a moment, never wanting to look back on the past or think of what might have happened. The big "what if" wouldn't change where they were now.

Caroline had done this to him. Coming back here, seeing her after all these years. Nothing more than two friends, but she'd stirred him up inside. *Lord*, he prayed. *I could use all the help I can get right now.*

Sometime later, he stood by the mailbox and waited as Bryson hopped down off the bus. He took Bryson's lunch box in one hand and held out the other for him. "Where did you go today?"

Sam closed his hand around Bryson's. He should have been asking how his son's day went, but his little dude beat him to it. "Mrs. Thompson needed her light fixed, and Rob needed help over at the tree farm."

Bryson, with his mother's sharp green eyes and Sam's thick black hair, wrinkled his nose. "Is that why you always smell like gram's car?"

"A lot better than cleaning Pap's barn." Sam led him into the small yellow house they rented on the far side of town.

Bryson turned his seven-year-old head to the side. "Pap has a barn?"

Sam shook his head. His kid had developed a bit of a sass since starting school. "You know what I meant."

"One day, I'm not going to be a farmhand. I'm not even going to own a farm. They smell." Sam's heart lurched. He'd said the same thing at Bryson's age. A certain peace filled him in this place. Home. This is where he came to raise his son. He couldn't think of any other place he would ever want to be. His family was here. His life was here.

And now Caroline was here.

Her eyes, the sound of her laugh, and her smile still lingered in his thoughts throughout the day.

What about the Christmas tree lot? If he's not doing anything there, why not send him home and have him wait for his son there?

I agree. Maybe just delete the part about the tree lot or have him go get a tree.

Chapter Three

After she'd gotten Duke settled and unpacked her things in her new room, Caroline went downstairs, glad when Aunt Marge returned. The old house was too big to be comfortable with one person mousing around inside.

"I'm sorry I wasn't here when you arrived, dear." Marge helped herself to the boiling water on the stove, which Caroline used to make a cup of tea, hoping her aunt would return soon. Duke walked around the house, investigating his new surroundings.

"I am. I took the room with the pink roses. I hope you don't mind."

Marge joined Caroline at the small, round breakfast nook by the window. She eased herself down onto a chair and sighed. "As I figured you would."

"Where did you go?" she asked, playing around with a cookie she still had on her plate after helping herself to a snack while her aunt was gone.

"Church. It's Wednesday and some of us retired folk like to get together. We've been working through a new Bible study. Ross James has been leading it now for a few weeks."

Caroline missed her own Bible study group. There didn't

seem to be enough time when she started working and Josh never would wait for her. He insisted she get a job, with him still in school taking classes toward his PhD, as they needed the income. He never missed church, or he hadn't at first. Then it seemed to separate them, and she found herself alone. Even the women at church stopped inviting her to events. She'd found Duke at a shelter. Those big puppy eyes had her falling in love at first sight. She'd taken him home to keep her company in the lonely evenings of Josh's absence. Caroline got a job, doing as Josh said, as he always had a way of making her feel guilty about not being a good wife.

She glanced over at Duke sniffing out the living room, pushing her failed marriage to the farthest part of her mind. God knew how hard she'd tried, and she'd held on for as long as she'd been able. It hadn't been enough. *She* hadn't been enough.

"This Sunday, we'll start lighting the candles. It's my favorite time of year." Aunt Marge reached over and took Caroline's ice-cold hand into her warmed ones, pulling Caroline's attention back. "I'm glad you and Duke came. You're welcome for however long you need. I know it was a hard decision not to go to your parents..."

"With Janelle there?" Caroline shook her head. "Besides, you know Dad. He would have never allowed Duke to stay in the house. And I'd much rather help you with all those centerpieces and Christmas swags you make."

Tasks. She needed to keep her hands busy enough not to let her heart cause her mind to have any more sadness plague it. Her life with Josh was over. No matter what he told others about how it ended or why, it no longer mattered. She'd come home. She'd avoided it for months after the divorce. Now she'd have to listen to all the "I told you so's" from her sisters.

"That reminds me, can you drive out to the Gavin farm in the morning and pick up some pine limbs for me?" Marge lifted her cup of steaming tea and relaxed back in her chair. "Driving on these winter roads doesn't appeal to me so much anymore."

"Sure. I haven't been there in a few years. Does Rob still give out axes to cut your own tree?"

"Oh, I think he does. Maybe you could pick out a tree for in the parlor and a smaller one for outside on the porch. Now that you're staying here, we can put up the greens on the posts. The red bows will need to be dusted off from the attic. How lovely it will be to have the house decked out for the season again. Perhaps we can have Sam come over and help put the lights up in the high places." Marge slid Caroline a glance and took another sip of her tea. She knew that devious look of her aunt's, and she wouldn't fall for it.

Caroline told her mother she would come home, but she never promised to stay. Hidden Hills was the last place she wanted to live again. She didn't feel she had a place here anymore. Her heart ached for the life she'd left back in the city, and a small part still stung from the man who'd pushed her away.

Outside, the winds picked up and rattled the old rain gutters above the windows. Duke padded into the kitchen, nosing around with the scents of peppermint wafting from the steam of their hot tea.

"I suppose if you're settled in, you could help me a bit in the shop. I've got orders piling in for the Snow Ball at the high school, and Mrs. McCleary over on Old Mill Road passed last Friday. I think I'm about out of those lovely red velvet roses I had to finish Jasper's boutonniere for his and Grace's anniversary party in the church's social hall next Saturday."

"You're using silk flowers?" Caroline remembered her own silk flowers for her wedding. She'd made them here with Aunt Marge. She tried to hold back her disappointment by walking into the flower shop connected to the front of the house.

"They're getting expensive, having to order the real ones all the time. I've got to run clear to Louisville to get them, and sometimes the greenhouse in Shelbyville has a few. This way I can order them and have them shipped right to the house." Marge scooted behind a table in the back part of the shop.

Caroline walked through the rest of the shop; wreaths had gotten dusty. Everything appeared out of season and dated, hanging on the wooden lattice on the walls, and bits and pieces of ribbon clippings and plastic stems littered the floor. Across the front entrance, Marge's parlor greeted her with its worn velvet lounge and winged back chair sitting by an empty fireplace.

She came back into the shop area and watched to see her aunt picking through the red velvet silk roses she'd mentioned.

"What about the greenhouse here in town? Don't they grow flowers anymore?"

Marge rested her hands on the table and looked over at Caroline. She frowned as she eased herself down into a metal fold-out chair. "We had a snowstorm a few years back. The greenhouse collapsed, but the insurance didn't give them enough to make it worth it to fix it or rebuild it. Now, Will Harrison's got a place over in Shelbyville. They got vegetables growing in the barn, I hear. And tanks with live trout."

"Then we'll add a greenhouse in the back here for you. It will be a lovely addition to the house and will add business." Caroline chewed on her lip. She shouldn't have said that. Staying here was a temporary thing until she got back on her feet again.

"You'd have to take care of it. I can't be going out all the time to tend the flowers. I don't have the money to keep stock like I once did, let alone add a greenhouse. Business isn't what it used to be anymore. A lot of folks must go out of town for most things. Few are splurging for flowers unless it's a funeral, or like me, they don't like to drive far to get things." Marge held up a silk rose bud as she spoke.

"We agreed I'd help you here in the shop in return for the room. We'll make some changes, do some advertising online, and people will come back." The first thing to do would be to fill these empty flower coolers.

"That's all fine if you want to do it. I can't keep up with it all anymore. Could you dig around in that bucket behind you and see if you could find me some baby's breath for these roses?"

While, Caroline searched, she noted an inventory list in her mind. Later, when her aunt napped in her room, Caroline rolled up her sleeves and got to work inside the flower shop. This had always been her favorite place. Even as a child, she loved to come to Aunt Marge's shop to watch her arrange the flowers and listen to her talk about the different types and how best to care for them to last longer for others to enjoy.

Caroline used the flower shop as an excuse when her sisters sent texts and told her to come over to their parents' house. *Too busy, catch you this weekend*. She couldn't avoid seeing her family forever. They wouldn't understand she needed time. Nor would they consider she needed to make her own decisions.

And seeing Samuel Brink again brought her only more confusion. She didn't expect seeing him would stir a feeling inside her she'd avoided since her divorce became finalized.

She pushed it back down where she couldn't feel it again. What were the chances she'd run into him again?

Chapter Four

THE WEATHERMAN PREDICTED SNOW FLURRIES OFF AND on throughout the day. Sam stomped his feet to wake his toes from their frost-bitten state inside his boots. He snipped another branch and tossed it on the sled. Rob had sent him out to trim up and cut some new stock to display outside his Christmas tree lot.

Sam looked at his stack on the sled before heading back to his truck parked up beside the road to load it. They'd gotten several inches of snow over the past week.

There in the lot beside his truck, he spied the little sedan. He almost tripped over his own two feet at the sight of the woman sliding out of the driver's seat. Her dark hair was pulled back in a ponytail, and her navy-blue coat with a bit of fur around her hood took him back almost ten years.

Friends, they'd been friends then, and he'd promised to be her friend now.

Swallowing hard, he trudged ahead. Raising his hand, he waved, heading right toward her. "Fancy seeing you here."

He wanted to smack himself at the choice of words. Fancy... She looked so... He sighed. She stood there, a deep frown on her face, looking like so many other people he remembered from living in the city. But this was Caroline. The sweet girl who laughed and talked with him on the bus. His queen of the back seats. And what he hadn't been able to see in her back then, he recognized coming up to stand in front of her.

"I didn't figure I'd see you here." She bit her lip, and he found it adorable.

"Just trimming some trees for Rob before another surge of people come on the weekend looking for their one special tree, you know."

"Not really," she shrugged. "My mom doesn't like real trees in the house."

"What?" He pretended to be affronted by her proclamation. "You sure she's Marge's sister?"

That brought a smile to Caroline's face and added a childish twinkle to her eyes. "Oh, don't you worry. I've got to tell Rob that Aunt Mar wants two this year, as always. Mom, however, doesn't like all the dead pine needles in the carpet of the family room, and the entire house smelling of pine isn't her thing."

"And what of you? What kind of tree will you be having this year?" It wasn't his place to ask, and he didn't mean to pry. Sam could have kicked himself for turning her smile upside down again. She lost the moment of sparkle in her eye.

"Real I suppose. Since I'm staying with Aunt Mar for the holidays." She tilted her head and looked at the branches in the sled behind him. "Are those cut branches?"

"Yes, ma'am. Rob asked me to trim some trees. It makes it easier for the city goers coming in to cut their own trees down. I was going to toss them on the back of my truck and take them over behind the barn to dispose of them."

Her hazel eyes widened. "Doesn't Rob sell them?"

"Who would buy them?" Sam pulled the sled up closer to his truck. Reaching for the tailgate, she stopped him.

"I would."

Looking down at her gloved hand on his arm, he held the tailgate from dropping. His pulse raced beneath her touch. He couldn't keep it from speeding up.

"You'd buy pine branches?"

Her cheeks turned pink. From the cold, he surmised, his gaze landing on the tip of her cute nose. What would it be like to drop a kiss there?

Quickly, as if she'd grabbed barbed wire, she jerked her hand away from him. "Well, with some ribbon and pinecones, I would. I mean, not like they are. I came hoping to get some to make swags and wreaths for Aunt Mar's shop."

And a sparkle came back into her eyes. In high school, she'd helped her aunt in the flower shop. She'd taken orders and made almost everyone's boutonnieres and corsages for their prom. If he remembered correctly, daisies were her favorite but would have to wait for spring to bloom.

"You do that, and Rob might want to sell them here in the barn when folks come to get trees."

Now the sparkle lit like flames in those swirling hazel eyes of hers, more green than blue with flecks of gold.

"Serious? That would be awesome!"

"Yeah. Help me put these in the back of my truck, and I'll drop them off over at Marge's later when I'm finished here."

"An electrician, farmer, tree trimmer, and delivery man. Is there anything you don't do?"

Sam waited until she stepped back, letting down the tailgate slowly. "What can I say? I'm a Jack of all trades."

"Indeed." Her eyes swept over him, and the wide spread of her smile brought warmth clear to his toes. For a moment, he considered asking her out to dinner. Too soon? Too fast?

It wasn't just him he needed to think about. He had a son. And even though Megan's betrayal didn't pain him as much anymore, it lingered every time he looked into the innocent eyes of his son. He'd moved too fast with Megan and hadn't really known her.

"Is there anything else I should know about you?"

"Lots. How about you?"

Together, they tossed the branches into the back of the truck.

The sun winked from above the barn, and he kept his back to the glare.

"Thanks to my sister, I'm sure you know more about my life than I do." Caroline rubbed her hands to get the pine needles off her gloves.

"She means well." Sam pushed up the tailgate as they finished. "I think sometimes folks gossip around here because they care about each other. Can't pray for one another if they don't know what needs to be fixed or healed, you know?"

She crossed her arms. "I never thought of it that way."

"Why don't we step in the barn a moment, grab some hot chocolate or coffee? I think you'll find Rob in the back wrapping up trees if you want to ask him about selling these fancy branches." He hitched his thumb to the back of the truck.

Caroline chewed on her bottom lip. He almost reached up to stop her when he caught sight of Rob coming out of the barn. "There's the man of the hour. I'd catch him before he heads off somewhere if I were you."

"Oh. Okay." She glanced over her shoulder. Rob must have heard his name, for he looked at her and waved. Caroline walked toward Rob.

"See you later," Sam called.

"Thanks!"

He didn't know what got into him. He took the sled and pulled it to the barn. Inside, he found the pot of hot coffee and leaned against the doorjamb. Caroline stood with Rob, her laughter floating across the barren parking lot. Rob grinned and nodded as Caroline spoke, her hands animating what she said. Sam let the warmth of the coffee spread through him. The heater at his feet worked to thaw his feet, but watching Caroline did something to him.

He had no business watching her like this, thinking of her like that. She wouldn't stay. As much as Janelle insisted her sister had come home, as much as Marge needed Caroline's assistance at the bed-and-breakfast, she would go.

She left straight from high school with big dreams of proving herself to the world. They all did. Big dreams. Huge ambitions. He never finished the police academy. Instead, he came home a father.

What would Caroline choose?

He watched her turn away, a bounce in her step as she returned to her car.

No, Caroline Adams could never be anything more to him than a friend. He couldn't even call her a high school sweetheart. She wasn't his then, and she could never be his now.

Rob walked back inside the barn. He didn't have to say it. Sam could see it on his pal's face.

"I heard she was back. Probably a good thing her sister is staying at her folks' place. Marge's been needing to get the shop back in order after all these years."

"You're starting to sound like her sister, Brenda."

Rob poured a cup of coffee and grabbed a container of powdered creamer. "Nothing wrong with a little hope. Sometimes all people need is a change of scenery to clear their thinking and direct them to what's important. Look at you."

"Says the one who never left," Sam pointed out.

"Because I was the smart one." Rob laughed. He took a gulp of hot coffee and hissed at the burn down his throat.

"You don't know what you're missing until you've left and come back." Sam put down his empty cup.

Rob grunted in response. Sam headed back outside, grabbed the sled rope, and turned toward the last tree he'd left his saw hanging on in the field. He'd pile Caroline high in pine branches, maybe enough to keep her in Hidden Hills past the new year.

Chapter Five

"There she is!"

"Mom? What are you doing here?" Caroline walked into the kitchen. Her mother, Dorothy, and sister, Brenda, sat at the table with Aunt Marge.

"You're just in time for tea. Sit." Aunt Marge pointed at an empty chair.

"Figured you weren't coming to see us, we'd come to see you," her mother said.

"Janelle said you were too busy for the likes of us." Brenda snickered over her cup of tea.

Caroline slipped off her jacket and hung it on the hook near the door. "That is not what I said."

She pulled out a chair about to take a seat and found Duke lying at Brenda's feet. *Traitor.* "Oh, no you don't. Out. Now."

Duke whined.

"Let him be." Dorothy motioned for her to sit.

"I'll not have him begging." He'd learned the bad habit from Josh. Determined to break it, she snapped her fingers, and Duke moved out from under the table. "Go lie down in the other room."

Caroline took him by the collar, his legs stiff in protest. The big brute whined again, but she pushed his body into the living room and pointed at the dog bed. He looked at her with those big dark eyes, and she sighed. "I'll make it up to you later."

Duke tilted his head, and she gave him a scratch under the saggy skin of his jaw.

Back in the kitchen, Aunt Marge stirred her tea. "He is no trouble in the kitchen. I don't mind."

"You don't understand, Aunt Marge. Poor Duke is the only man she's got left to boss around," Brenda said with a smirk.

It took all Caroline had inside her to bite back the remark on the tip of her tongue.

"Did you get any branches?" Aunt Marge asked.

Caroline took a cup and poured herself some tea. "Sam has them on the back of his truck. He'll drop them by later."

"Sam is such a sweet young man." Dorothy reached for a piece of pumpkin bread on the platter between them. Caroline didn't miss the look on her mother's face and wouldn't let it bother her. Her sisters and mother could play matchmaker all they wanted. Perhaps Brenda had been more right than she knew about men. Duke was the only male she needed to deal with this Christmas, but something told her to be careful. Not the look between her family, but the flutter in her stomach thinking of Samuel Brink.

"I hope he brings Bryson with him. I've missed him since school started."

"Bryson?" Caroline snapped to attention. Too late, Brenda grinned. She'd heard the octave of surprise in Caroline's voice.

"Sam's son. Didn't Janelle tell you?" Brenda reached for a slice of the sweet bread.

"No. I actually didn't know Sam was here until I came to Aunt Marge's."

"You could have come home," Caroline's mother said.

"And make Brenda share the room?"

Brenda snorted. "Not on your life."

"You could always move over here with Aunt Marge,"

Dorothy suggested to Brenda. Her younger sister snorted at the thought.

Caroline could see the flicker of hope in her mother's eyes. Her parents wanted her home, and she loved them for it. But she needed her space to find where she belonged again. Having Brenda in her old room brought up painful memories Caroline had left back in Louisville. How long would it take for Brenda to rub it in her face? She'd failed once again. Failed her marriage, failed her job, and failed the expectations of her family.

"I charge rent," Aunt Marge said. "Caroline's here helping with the shop. She'll have it back up and running full time before Christmas, I imagine."

Caroline's heart skipped a beat. "I never... I didn't..." She glanced between her mother's smiling face and Brenda's amused one. Aunt Marge sipped her tea and sat back in her chair. "It's alright, dear. Brenda here can come over and pitch in. We'll have those swags and wreaths made up enough for the craft bazaar at the church in a few weeks."

Caroline took a big gulp of her tea.

"Maybe at the craft bazaar, but I've got to work. *Some* of us have to work for a living." Brenda shivered. "Besides, Caroline is the crafty one. She's got nothing else to do."

Taking another sip of tea, Caroline turned toward Aunt Marge and ignored her sister. Like always, their mother paid no heed to the snide remark. Caroline put down her cup and reached for a piece of pumpkin bread before it was gone. She saw Duke's head peek around the doorway. He woofed.

"I need to take him out." She pushed back from the table and put her coat on. Slipping the piece of bread in her pocket, she reached for the leash by the door.

"You just got here, and now you're running off again," Brenda said.

"I suppose it does no good to wait for you to come back," her mother said.

"I'll be over on Wednesday to make pies and help prepare for Thanksgiving."

Duke came around the table and barked again. He danced near the door, and she took him by the collar long enough to snap on the leash. "I talked to Rob while I was over for the branches. He's going to hang the swag and wreaths to sell in the Christmas barn for us."

Her aunt lifted her teacup. "That's our girl, Dorothy. Louisville is probably sorry she's gone."

"Louisville," Dorothy said, referring to the nickname they'd given her ex-husband, Josh, "Isn't ever getting her back."

Just then, Duke gave the leash a jerk, and Caroline took him out.

Staying in the backyard didn't satisfy Duke's needs. He pulled her along down the snow-dusted sidewalks in town. Several blocks later, his gait slowed, and they fell into an easy step alongside each other. "You didn't need out for the reason you made me think, did you?"

Or maybe, just maybe, she'd taken his first bark at a sign of escape. She reached into her pocket and gave him the piece of pumpkin bread. In no hurry to return to Aunt Marge's place, they headed for another loop around town.

Down by the gas station, she spotted a truck like Sam's. "He's got a son, which probably means he has a wife." But the owner of the truck wasn't Sam. And she hadn't realized she stood there staring at the truck until Duke lifted a paw against her leg, looking up at her in wait. "He's only a friend."

Chapter Six

"Have a good day at school?" Sam brushed the top of Bryson's head as the boy hopped down off the school bus.

"Not really." Bryson swung his pack around on his back. "Mrs. Morrison gave us homework."

"Sounds rough. I guess you'll have to sit inside Marge's and work on it while I unload these pine branches from the back of my truck." What Sam suspected as a pout on his son's face evaporated into a sly grin.

"Marge's? You think she'll have more raisin cookies?"

Sam opened the door of his truck and motioned for Bryson to climb in. "I don't know Bud, but we're not going to ask her. We're going over so I can unload these pine branches for her and Caroline."

"Whose Caroline?" Bryson asked as Sam shut the door. He waited until he got in on his own side and Bryson had buckled his seatbelt. "She's Marge's niece. She's staying with Marge for the holiday."

"Is she my age? Will she be coming to school?" Bryson's brows furrowed. "Will I have to share my sugar cookies?"

Sam laughed, turning his head to look behind him as he

backed out of the driveway. "I don't think you have anything to worry about, Bry. Caroline and I went to school together."

"So... she's like your age?" Bryson asked.

Sam dared a quick glance at his son. He knew by the sound of Bryson's voice something churned in the six-year-old's head. "Yeah. And she's younger than Marge, so no questions about age. Women don't care about revealing that stuff. Got it?"

Bryson sat back in the truck seat and grinned. "Sure Dad, but if she's as old as you, then that means you and her can hang out, right?"

Sam hung a left and headed toward Main Street to Marge's. "It's not like the play dates you have with your friends, Bry. You just can't ask a girl to 'hang out'."

Bryson crossed his arms and looked over at him. "Why not? You hang out with Rob and Luke sometimes."

"That's different." He tried to change the subject. "What kind of homework did Mrs. Morrison give you?"

"How different?"

Sam groaned inwardly. This part of parenthood he would never be prepared for—the explaining things. Kids were always curious and Bryson amongst the most of them. There was no doubt in Sam's mind, Bryson needed a woman in his life, and not just a grandmother.

"Rob and Luke aren't girls. Caroline's a girl." *A beautiful girl.*

"Then you should ask her out on a date."

Sam almost drove past the bed and breakfast as he looked at Bryson and did not pay attention to the road. He tapped the brakes quick and swung around the turn to the bed and breakfast side parking. "A date?"

Bryson hit the button on his seatbelt and grabbed his backpack. "Jimmy says his mom goes out on dates all the time. Why can't you?"

"Well, for one..." The words were lost to him. Bryson arched his brow much like Sam's mother did and Sam shook his head. "We're friends. Just friends."

"Whatever." Bryson got out of the truck and Sam walked him up to Marge's front door. He hit the doorbell and Caroline came to answer.

"Hello there." She said to Bryson. Behind her, a Golden Retriever poked its head out around her leg. He'd seen the dog with Caroline the day she arrived at Marge's.

Caroline's eyes widened as Sam came up to stand behind his boy and place his hand on Bryson's shoulder. "Caroline, this is my son, Bryson."

"You're Caroline?" Bryson hooked his backpack over his shoulder.

"Bry, mind your manners."

Caroline glanced up at Sam a moment before gazing back down at his son. "I am, and this furry guy behind me trying to meet you is my dog, Duke."

"Oh, cool!" Bryson reached out, then stopped. "Can I pet him?"

"Sure, but don't let him knock you down. Duke doesn't have a lot of experience around kids." Caroline stepped aside. She held onto Duke's collar. "Be nice," she told the dog.

Funny, Sam almost said the same thing to Bryson.

"You don't got no kids." Bryson said, more of a statement than a question. Sam couldn't help noticing the way Caroline flinched.

She put on a sweet smile, standing there in her oversized college sweatshirt and a pair of snug jeans. She ran her hand down over the dog, whose tail swung back and forth behind her. "No kids, but I've got Duke. He's kind of like my kid."

"Hey Dad. She doesn't have a kid and we don't have a dog."

"Yeah, bud." He heard, and he didn't know if Caroline was looking for one either. Sam tugged his hat down further on his head. It hasn't escaped him she hadn't invited them in yet.

Bryson pressed past her to pet the dog. It didn't take long before Bryson shoved his way half into the house with the dog following behind before Caroline turned away.

Sam laid a hand on her arm. "Sorry. He's been here so many times I guess he feels right making himself at home."

She'd let her hair down. The ends tickled against his hand. She glanced at his hand, and he let it drop away, then her hazel gaze met his. She'd put on a pair of black-rimmed glasses since he'd seen her earlier in the day. He liked them. They suited her. He would have told her to wear them more often, but he didn't know how she'd receive the compliment. Some women got funny about those things. He didn't know if Caroline would. He realized he knew the Caroline of the past, but not much of the Caroline of the present. If he was going to make it a point to become friends, he probably should ask her out for coffee or something.

Her face flushed a little, and she stepped back when he heard Marge's voice in the other room with Bryson.

"I heard 'cookies.' Do you want to come in?"

"She spoils him worse than my Mom," Sam chuckled.

"She always did us, too." Caroline moved out of the way for him to enter. "I'm sure she has enough for us all. I don't know what Aunt Mar would do if she wasn't baking or arranging flowers."

Tempted by her offer, drawn to step closer to her, Sam held off. He couldn't allow his thoughts, his feelings, to tangle around a woman who had recently untied the knot with someone else. He cleared his throat. "I came to deliver the pine branches before it got dark. Bryson's got homework. Is it okay if he works on it in here while I unload the truck? Marge rarely minds him here when I'm fixing something, and he stays with her occasionally when Ma's got to stay late at the doctor's office."

"His mother is at work?"

Sam didn't enjoy talking about Bryson's mother. "Megan's not in the picture."

"Oh." Caroline shifted from one foot to the other.

Sam tipped his hat, the cold nipping at his jeans. "I'd best get that unload."

About to step off the porch, Caroline said, "Wait. Give me a minute and I'll come out and help you."

Outside, Sam put down the tailgate and together he and Caroline unloaded the branches. She showed him where to pile them around the side of the house, and the last armful she opened the door to the floral shop on the side of the old house, directing him inside.

Someone had come in and started dissecting parts of the store. The floral refrigerators were pulled out from the wall and unplugged. Tables and inventory piled and shoved to the left side of the shop. The counter, an old countertop bar, sat in two pieces. Sam whistled as he laid down the branches.

"It's been a while since the place had a good cleaning. Aunt Mar's open to changing things around a bit, too." She dusted her hands off from the pine needles they'd laid on a table beside her.

"Is that what you did in the city?"

She clasped her hands in front of her. "Actually, I worked at the University in the administrative offices."

"Worked? Not work?"

She laughed uncomfortably, and he hated to make her feel that way. He shouldn't have pried. Janelle never mentioned what Caroline did. He figured it was better to find out from her, get it straight, and be a good friend.

"I quit after the divorce." She put her finger to her lips. Glancing around at them, she allowed the finger to slide down. He couldn't seem to look anywhere but at those sweet, berry-glossed lips.

"Shh... our secret, okay?"

Sam crossed his arms. "Okay..."

Then she laughed again. "Aunt Mar knows, but no one else. If I tell my family, they'll expect me to stay. And..." she shrugged. "I'm not sure where I'm going from here. At least for now, they think I've just taken my vacation time before the semester break, so I have until the New Year."

He moved closer, unable to resist from the spooked look in

her eyes. She'd dropped her voice to a mere whisper as she spoke. He leaned in, drew her close, and whispered in her ear. "Your secret is safe, me Caroline. I can't say I understand what you're feeling or what you're going through, but I'm here." Then his next words hurt, caused an ache in him he couldn't explain. "I'm your friend."

She relaxed against him, wrapped her arms around him in a hug. He would have gladly died a lucky man should he never be close to her again.

"Thank you, Sam. That means more to me than you'll ever know."

But he already did, and this friend thing just got more complicated as he didn't want to let her go.

Chapter Seven

WEDNESDAY MORNING CAME WITHOUT A WINK OF SNOW in the forecast. Caroline arrived at her childhood home long after the baking started. Stepping into the kitchen, she could smell the pumpkin pies in the oven. On the table, Janelle worked on rolling out a pie crust while Brenda stood at the sink cleaning out their mother's prize mixing bowl to use again.

Caroline put the groceries on the butcher block counter.

"I see how you are." Janelle laughed. "Show up after we're almost done."

"The store didn't open until nine. Aunt Mar said you called and needed cinnamon and chocolate pudding."

"You could have run to Shelbyville where the Walmart is," Brenda pointed out. Janelle waved her hand. "It doesn't matter. You're here now, so you can clean up."

Caroline tried to stop from rolling her eyes. Of course, she got stuck with cleanup.

"Where's that dog of yours?" her mother asked. "You know your father won't allow it in the house."

"I left Duke with Aunt Mar," she said.

"You still don't want to come here and stay?" Brenda asked teasingly.

"And room with you?" Caroline tried to tease back. "I think I told you the room was yours when I left."

"It's still your room, too," their mother told Caroline.

"Yeah, but there's only one bed, and I've got my desk and my drawing table all set up," Brenda complained. She'd gone to college for four years, came home, and was working online as a virtual assistant. If all else failed, Caroline had put it on her list of future job options. Although, later, she planned to ask Brenda if she liked it and how much it paid. She needed to make enough money to go back to the city, to her church there, and move on with her life.

No matter how many pies they made and stacked up on the counter, Caroline couldn't wait for them to finish so she could clean up and go back to Aunt Marge's. Duke would need to go for a walk, and she wanted to work on some of the pine branches Sam delivered.

"Don't worry," Caroline assured her, watching their mother roll out the dough for another pie crust. "I am happy at Aunt Mar's. Duke wouldn't like being kept outside, and besides, I need to make a bunch of swags and wreaths for the Christmas tree farm before tomorrow if we're going to sell any. Do you think I could get some baler twine from the barn?" Caroline asked her mother.

"I don't think your father would care. He's got a bunch hanging off the peg by the doors at the top of the barn." Dorothy sprinkled flour on the dough. "Marge said you were cleaning and rearranging the shop. You should ask Sam to help you. He's handy with a hammer."

"Oh, yes!" Janelle chimed in, dumping another dirty bowl in the sink for Caroline to wash. "You should have him build you some display shelves for that far wall and move the sales counter there. You can put your centerpiece displays back there and hang some wreaths and swags between the windows and door."

"Then where will she get anything done if she moves that to the back? Aunt Marge always kept that as her workspace where people could watch her create their orders," Brenda pointed out.

"I think people like that," their mother interjected. "It adds that personal touch, and you can make my order then."

"I think so, too." For once, she agreed with her mother. "The shop isn't that big, so I was hoping to balance the space. Aunt Mar says business has been down."

"You could set up the shop online." Brenda picked up the pudding supplies as it wouldn't be a holiday pie-making day without chocolate cream pie. "I could make you a website."

"You could…" Caroline said, slowly.

"Oh, let her make you a website." Their mother placed the dough in a pie dish and slid it to Janelle.

"It wouldn't be a website for me," Caroline balked.

"Yes, it would. Aunt Mar's arthritis is getting too bad for doing flower arrangements. Consider the website my Christmas gift." Brenda reached for the meringue off a cooling pie, and their mother slapped at Brenda's hand. "Those are for Thursday."

"But that's like two days away."

Janelle rolled her eyes. "You'll survive. Just like Caroline will survive being back home again. Don't think for a moment we can't see it on your face that you don't want to be here."

Caroline put the bowl she was washing on the rack. "I said nothing."

"You don't have to say anything." Her mother sighed. "He didn't deserve you. He promised me he would take care of you, and he lied. You're home now. This is where you belong."

"I have a life," Caroline said. "I can't give up everything and move because of Josh."

Her mother sucked in a breath.

"Don't say his name. It's like a bad word around here," Brenda informed her.

"I don't know why you'd want to go back. There's nothing in the city for you." Janelle opened the oven and placed the new pies inside.

"How about her job?" Brenda supplied.

"She can find one like you did," their mother said. "But if she wants to go back, we can't stop her. Just know, Carrie, if you do, it'll break your father's heart."

It didn't escape her notice how her mother pulled out her emotional weaponry by calling her by the nickname her father had given her since birth and mentioned him. Eventually, she'd have to have a talk with her father. She'd find him out in the barn fixing the tractor or feeding the cows. Out of all of them, he was probably the smartest, avoiding the kitchen on baking day.

"And you've already been married to a city guy and seen how they treat their wives. You won't find a man like, say, Sam Brink, in the city. He at least knows how to fix things." Janelle grinned.

Caroline tossed her hand towel at her sister, but Janelle laughed and set the timer on the stove. "For that, you can finish the dishes on your own."

"Do you think we have enough pies?" asked their mother, glancing around with the rolling pin in her hand.

"Unless you're taking a few to the church dinner on Sunday, we have more than enough," Janelle said.

"Maybe we should make another lemon," their mother suggested, with a spot of flour on her cheek. Her dark hair curled against one side of her face.

"We don't need more lemon or any other flavor. Why don't you go clean up and relax before Dad comes in from the barn?" Janelle steered their mother out of the kitchen. Glancing back, she gave Caroline a hard stare. Caroline understood that look and shook her head. She wouldn't let her sister intimidate her. One more reason staying here was a bad idea.

Brenda offered to help clean up the mess. As she cleared the counters and the table, Caroline finished washing the dishes. They chatted, mostly about the website and ideas to get the shop running again. While Janelle always had an eye for interior design, Brenda loved her to-do lists and helping others.

"I can start on it later," Brenda said. "Make sure you take pictures of your creations so we can use them on the site. I set up a site for Rob, too, last year. He doesn't sell online, but it lets people find his business and have a point of contact. We can get you set up to sell, and we can also put your stuff up on some other sites. I can show you how."

"It's not my shop." Caroline watched the timer on the stove when they'd finished. "You'll have to ask Aunt Mar if she wants all that."

"You should consider quitting your job. Aunt Mar's health has been declining. She likes to spend most of her days at the library with Aunt Maeve instead of at her place. I think she's lonely. She asked me once if I wanted to move in with her after I came home from college so I could run the B&B. Hospitality isn't one of my gifts. You, on the other hand…" Brenda shrugged. "And don't let Janelle go pushing Sam on you. The man's got his own problems, and I doubt he's looking for a wife."

"I see." Caroline sank into a chair at the table.

Brenda glanced around the doorway leading into the living room. She walked over, snatched the dollop of baked meringue off the top of the lemon pie, and plopped it in her mouth. Caroline stared at her for a moment.

"What?" Brenda asked, her mouth still full.

Caroline shook her head. "I didn't say a word."

Chapter Eight

Sam received the call at nine in the morning to pick up Bry from school. He'd planned to spend his morning at the pig farm, then after lunch, head to the Christmas tree farm to stack cut trees against the barn to help Rob. School would let out two hours early to dismiss the kids for Thanksgiving break, and his mother had a full shift at the doctor's office. His father offered to take Bryson into Shelbyville with him to see a man about an antique truck he wanted to restore. His father liked to repair old vehicles when he wasn't tinkering with them at the repair shop in town where he worked.

By ten, Sam had Bryson in his truck and cuddled against him. "We'll have to see if you can stay with Marge for a few hours until I finish at the pig farm. I'll have to call Rob and tell him I can't work this afternoon."

"No!" Bryson cried. His little cheeks were red and flushed with fever. He sniffed, pressing a gloved hand to his runny nose. "Why can't I stay with Mar? Isn't that other lady there too? You know the nice one with the dog?"

"Caroline, and probably. But you can't stay with Mar and have her take care of you all day. I have to fix the gate at the farm and feed the pigs, then I'll be back to get you. We can't expect Mar to take care of you all the time, and you might make her sick."

Bryson closed his eyes. Sam could feel the heat radiating off the boy. He called his mother at the doctor's office, and she reported the flu was going around, their office busy with people coming in all day. He stopped at the store to grab Pedialyte and popsicles, along with the other suggested items his mother told him.

Marge owned the largest house in the middle of town, just down the street from the little library. The stairs to the big wide porch lead to the door of the front room which housed her little floral shop. Farther down, on the side, was the formal entrance used by the guests of the B&B with the large wide foyer and table displaying the guest book and pen for people to sign in. But according to Marge, Sam was no longer a guest, so he and Bryson used the back door, going into the kitchen. He knocked first, hearing no one. He ushered Bryson inside. "Hello?"

Bryson moved inside, and Sam stepped past him, putting popsicles in the freezer and setting the rest down on the table. A moment later, a woof and the sound of paws thundering from the other room caused him to back up and push Bryson behind him. The boy clung to his father, then leaned out around to peer as the big Golden Retriever skidded to a halt. "Woof, Woof," Duke greeted them.

"See, Dad. He knows us. He won't hurt us."

"Duke!"

Sam allowed Bryson to step around him, and the Golden Retriever licked the boy's face. Bryson went down on his knees and petted the big dog.

"What on..." Caroline came into the kitchen, a hammer in hand and her beautiful eyes widened behind those black-framed glasses.

"Sorry. Marge allows us to come right in."

Slowly, Caroline lowered the hammer. "You've been here over three times."

Sam reached back and cupped the back of his neck. "Yep."

Marge Adams had a rule. First time you're a guest, second you're a pest, and the third and after you were family. Family could come right in, according to the older woman.

"Aunt Mar isn't here. She's at the library and then was going to her Wednesday afternoon Bible study."

"I forgot. Today is Wednesday." He reached for his phone. He would have to call Elmer at the pig farm and tell him the gate would have to wait and he'd have to feed the pigs on his own today. Before he could hit the call button, Bryson coughed. Duke woofed, and Caroline sat her hammer on the table to rub Bryson's back.

She looked at Sam, the concern in her eyes gripping him in the way she cared about his son. "I take it we're having a sick day?"

"The school called. Mom's at work, and Dad left for Shelbyville early this morning. I hoped Marge would be here, and Bry could stay a few hours while I got my work done over at the pig farm."

He watched her face, waiting for the slightest change. She frowned as Bryson coughed. "Well, I guess it's the couch for you, kid," Caroline said. "There is a blanket on the end. Don't let Duke on the couch. He's a blanket hog, and if you watch anything with other dogs, he'll bark at them."

"Are you sure?" Sam asked, uncertain whether to leave his son or call off.

Caroline reached for Bryson's coat and helped him out of it. She held out her hand, and Bryson gave her his gloves. "Off you go," Caroline pointed in the living room's direction. Duke tilted his head. "You too," she told him. "Stay with Bryson."

Duke followed the boy.

"Hey Bry," Sam said, his throat clogging.

A ruddy-cheeked boy with messy hair glanced back at him.

"Rest and don't cause Caroline any trouble."

Bryson nodded before he left.

"I really appreciate this," Sam said. "I got soup, and there are popsicles I put in the freezer. Medicine here on the table. Mom said every four hours for the fever and if he...."

Caroline laid a hand on his arm, stopping him from saying more. "I may not have kids of my own, Sam, but it'll be okay. Go so you can get back. I'll take good care of him. He'll be on the couch, and Duke will watch over him. Aunt Marge has like a hundred channels on the television for him to pick from, unless you don't want him to watch television."

"Television is fine, just nothing inappropriate." He swallowed hard, his gaze on those slim fingers resting on his arm.

"I wouldn't let a young kid watch anything we adults do, and even then, I don't think anything Aunt Mar and I like to watch is hazardous to a kid's viewing. Last night, it was that old movie *White Christmas*. You can trust me with your son."

"I do," he said and meant it.

Before Caroline's hand could slip off his arm, he gripped it with his free one. "Most people wouldn't want to deal with someone else's sick kid."

"I'm not someone else." She covered her hand over his again, stacking their hands together.

No, she was his queen of the back seats and the girl he'd always admired. She knew what she wanted, and she hadn't been afraid to go after it. His gaze landed on their hands. "Caroline."

"Go."

"I owe you one."

She grinned, and his gaze followed the movement of her mouth. Caroline lifted her hands from his as he tried to hold on to them and failed, too distracted by thoughts of what it would be like to kiss her.

"When you get back, maybe you can help me build some shelves for the shop." She picked her hammer back up.

That caught his attention. "Shelves?"

"I was told you're the best handyman in town," she grinned.

"For you, I'd do anything," he said.

Caroline clutched the hammer and stepped back. He shouldn't have said it. A flash of uncertainty crossed her features. He grinned, trying to play it off. "Thanks again for watching over Bryson."

"What are friends for?"

Chapter Nine

Caroline spent the morning setting up a table and working on tying together branches and making swags. She peeked in on Bryson while the young boy lay on the couch. He fell asleep an hour after his father dropped him off. Duke rested in front of the couch, catching her gaze. His head would pop up, and she'd press her finger to her lips. Several times, she watched the boy sleep. Once she'd pulled down a crocheted blanket around the boy, seeing him shiver. Pressing her hand against his head to feel the warmth, she kept a glass of water nearby and a bowl in case he got worse.

How many times had she asked Josh about having a baby? He always put her off with excuses for time. "We have plenty of time, babe." Or he'd ask her, "Don't you have some things you'd like to do before taking care of a baby? You won't be able to have a career and stay at home," he'd say. Having a career and a family never conflicted with the future she envisioned. She'd gone to college to get a business degree. All her life, she had wanted to have a business of her own and to raise a family. When she met Josh, she thought God had answered her prayers. He'd brought her a man who shared her faith, was working on a career to support them, and said he wanted children. What he really wanted was a wife to support his love of learning for him to be a lifelong student.

Her heart ached at all the disagreements. When she'd brought Duke home, he confessed he thought she would stop wanting a family and settle into her administrative role at the college. Josh heard about the job and insisted she apply. It helped him to save on the cost of tuition.

Caroline cut more branches, letting the smell of the pine soothe her through those memories. "What do you want me to do?" she whispered.

Duke came to the doorway and whined. "What's up, boy?"

Looking at the clock, she realized it was nearly noon. He needed to go for a walk, but she couldn't leave Bryson. "Sorry, boy. You'll have to go out in the yard." She padded quietly down the hall, checking on Bryson. At the back door, she took hold of the line and clipped it to Duke's collar. The Golden Retriever whined again as she opened the door. "At least it's not snowing," she said.

Duke headed out the door. She picked up the can of soup Sam had left on the table and wrinkled her nose. Checking through the cupboards, Caroline set out to make lunch. By the time she had the carrots chopped and the noodles in the pot with the broth, a scratch sounded at the door followed by a "woof."

As she opened the door, the knob turned and pushed her back. Sam stepped through the doorway, followed by Duke, restrained by the line clipped to his collar. Caroline stepped back, hitting the kitchen table. Sam reached out to steady her as Duke yanked and barked to come inside.

"I am sorry. I didn't see you." He held on, looking at her with those stormy eyes. He wore a pair of Carhart overalls and a jacket. The cap on his head beaded with water from the heat of the kitchen, melting the snow.

Snow! It must have snowed again after she let Duke out. Hurriedly, she moved around Sam. "Duke, sit!"

Sam spun around too, taking two strides to reach the dog

before she could get to him. He unsnapped the line and let Duke in before closing the door. "Didn't forget about you," Sam said.

"Hold on to him," Caroline told Sam. "Don't let go of his collar yet." She moved to the hook by the door and grabbed a towel she kept there for Duke. Hunching down, one paw at a time, she wiped off the Golden Retriever's feet. Sam hunched down with her, keeping hold of Duke. "Guess this isn't his first rodeo?"

"No." Caroline toweled the next foot. "I tried buying those boots for him, but he chews them off and hates them."

"A dog that doesn't like boots."

Caroline looked over at him.

He grinned.

"Okay, all done."

Sam released Duke, and the dog took off again for the living room.

"He hasn't left Bryson's side all morning," Caroline explained. "He fell asleep a little while ago, but I'm sure you'll want to check on him."

"I should take him and go home," Sam said.

"No." Panic flared inside of Caroline. "Please. Stay. I've started making lunch, and you really don't want to wake him, do you?"

Sam scratched his chin. A bit of growth there she hadn't noticed earlier drew her gaze along his strong jawline.

"I don't want to burden you any further." He shifted his weight.

"You still owe me those shelves, remember? Take off your coat and have lunch. Bryson is resting. And you don't want to make me have to eat all this soup I'm making on my own, do you?" She made a pleading face. Pouting. Blinking to flick her lashes up and down.

Sam reached for the zipper of his jacket. "When you put it that way, how can I refuse?"

Caroline laughed, something loosening in her chest, almost freeing for the first time in ages.

"Show me where you want those shelves, and I'll work on them while you work on lunch."

He went back outside, walking around to the big wide porch and coming in through the front of the shop so he wouldn't track snow through the house. After pulling out her phone and showing him the Pinterest picture for inspiration, he shook his head with amusement.

"Let me see your phone," he said.

Chapter Ten

Caroline hesitated. Sam quirked his brow, his hand out. "You want the shelves, don't you?"

Pinching her lips together, she handed over the phone. She watched with a twisting in her gut as he swiped his fingers across her phone screen, enlarging the picture. His eyes fixed on the photo. She moved a little closer, leaning in to see what he viewed. Then quickly, he shrunk the picture, hit the little icon to share it, and sent it to himself. He gave her back her phone. "Now I have the photo, and you have my number for future reference."

Her fingers tingled as they brushed against his for that slight moment of taking back her phone. Her breath eased out as she hadn't realized she'd been holding it during the exchange. "Your number?"

"Text me. Call me." He shrugged. "I want to check on Bry, then I'll see what I can do about your vision for in here. I can probably help with the rest if you're wanting to make it like the picture, or do you want only the shelves?"

"Only the shelves." Caroline glanced around the quaint little shop space. "I have a few other pictures for more ideas. I wanted to paint the walls cream and the shelves to be stained dark wood. Dad said he has some old barn wood I could use. I brought a few pieces over." She pointed to the floor where she'd measured and planned.

"You work on the soup. Leave the shelves for me. If you send me the other pictures, I can help you."

Caroline pressed the phone against her heart. "I can't ask you to do all that. The shelves would be a great help. I can manage the rest on my own."

Sam looked at her for a long moment, then nodded.

She returned to her food preparations and left him to check on Bryson. Later, as she stirred the soup, a blurry-eyed little boy staggered into the kitchen. Duke followed dutifully behind.

"Hey there," Caroline said, softly.

"Where's my dad?" Bryson asked.

"He's working out in the shop. I was about to go get him for some soup. Do you think you can eat? Are you hungry?"

Bryson rubbed his eyes. "A little."

"How do you feel?" She reached over, touching his forehead, and grimaced. Poor kid still felt warm.

"My chest hurts." Bryson covered his mouth as he coughed.

"Does it hurt when you cough?" she asked.

Bryson nodded.

"Okay." Caroline smoothed away a piece of his hair against his forehead. "Hopefully, some good ole chicken soup will help make it better. My mother made it for us when we didn't feel good either."

"Your mom?" Bryson asked, his voice hoarse. Caroline glanced past him in search of Sam. She wrapped her arm around Bryson and steered him back to the couch.

"It was my grandmother's recipe, but my gram died before I was born, so I never met her. My mom said she made the same soup for her and making it helps keep my gram's memory alive for my mom."

"Doesn't that make her sad?" Bryson coughed again.

"A little, I suppose, but I also think it makes her happy that she can share that with her kids and pass it along."

"Are you going to do the same for your kids?" Bryson asked as he hopped back onto the couch, and Caroline sat beside him. Duke sat at the end of the couch near the coffee table. She'd been afraid if she turned off the television that the lack of background noise might wake the boy up while he'd been napping.

"Yep. But first I need to have some." She pulled out her phone and texted Sam. The soup was done, and Bryson was awake. Without Bryson seeing, she also typed in her concern about his cough. She knew Sam's mother was a nurse for the doctor here in town and probably would give him better advice than she could. Looking over at Bryson, she put on her best smile to hide the worry.

"You can be my mom," Bryson said. "I got a gram, but I don't have a mom."

"Bryson," Sam's voice startled them both.

Caroline held up her hand to Sam. "It's okay, really." Then she turned to Bryson. "I am honored you'd think of me that way. You're here because your mother brought you into this world. I wouldn't ever want to take her place when it doesn't belong to me."

Bryson curled up on the couch. Before Sam could approach the boy, she tugged on his arm and pulled him toward the kitchen. "I'm not an expert, but I think you should take Bryson to see your mother or to the nearest clinic. His cough is terrible."

"I appreciate your concern, Caroline. Kids get sick, and it always seems worse than it is."

"Plus, you've got your mom," Caroline said, trying to assure herself more than Sam. Bryson wasn't her kid, but after he'd asked her to be his mom, it made an ache in her chest reopen. How many years had she wasted with Josh waiting and yearning for a family? A family Josh never intended to make with her.

Turning away, Caroline took a deep breath to keep the build-up of tears from spilling over.

"Yeah, Mom has already texted a few times asking about him. I'll let her know about your concern."

Caroline could only nod. She reached for a bowl and the ladle, scooping first a bowl for Bryson and setting it off to the side to cool. She ladled another bowl and handed it back to Sam without looking in his direction.

"Thanks." He took the bowl, but she felt his nearness at her back. Her hand shook a little, holding the ladle. Sam sat down his bowl. As she turned, he caught her by the shoulders.

"You don't like chicken soup?" she asked.

"I don't like that you're upset. What happened? Did I do something?"

She stared down at the steaming soup. They'd have plenty of leftovers for the next few days. Aunt Marge expected guests later this evening for the Thanksgiving holiday. Caroline still had to double check the rooms to make sure they were prepared before Aunt Marge got back. She didn't want her aunt having to do it when it kept Caroline occupied, as if the shop wasn't enough.

"Caroline... Carrie."

Using her nickname had her allowing him to turn her in his arms. He searched her face, her spine stiffening at his assessment. Josh often scrutinized her each morning before she went to work. She learned to wear slacks and conservative blouses. Packing up and coming back to Hidden Hills, she'd left those things in boxes and found her old t-shirts, sweaters, and jeans.

"You did nothing, Sam. Bryson is your son. You know what is best for him. If you want to take him home, the shelves can wait until after Thanksgiving. We have guests coming this evening, and I have to get the rooms prepared before Aunt Marge tries doing it herself."

"You're right. I am Bryson's father." Sam's thumbs rubbed against her shoulders, causing little swirls of sensation that eased the straightness in her spine. "He shouldn't have said that to you about being his mother."

"I don't mind." She sagged some more as his fingers gripped her a little tighter, and she realized what she'd said. "I mean... Not that you and I would... I mean I wouldn't want to take his mom's place, like I said, but I...."

Sam placed a finger over her mouth. "Bryson never met his mother. Megan took off the moment the hospital cleared her to leave. She never looked back, never contacted me, even though I haven't changed my number."

Heart thumping in her chest, she waited for him to lower his finger and said, "I'm sorry. That must have been tough for you both."

"We weren't married." Sam stepped away. "Will you sit with me and talk after I take Bryson some soup?"

"I can do it." She reached for the bowl, then stopped. "Sure. I'll take our bowls to the dining room, where you can see him through the doorway."

While Caroline set the table with their bowls of soup, her cell phone rang. Recognizing the number from the university, she answered.

"Mrs. Lawlor, this is Hanna from HR."

"Adams." Caroline glanced in the living room's direction. She moved toward the kitchen. "I'm no longer married."

"My apologies. Your application said Lawlor."

"Application?"

"Yes, the Dean of Admissions has an opening for a secretary. It would be similar duties as your old job." Hanna explained as Caroline placed her hand flat down on the cool countertop near the stove. "If this is something that interests you, it would be an instant hire since you are still in our system from prior employment. You weren't fired, so I can process the paperwork upon your acceptance."

"It would have the same pay and benefits as my old position?" Caroline curled her hand into a fist. Her chest tightened at the prospect.

"It would. You would need to start right after the holidays."

"Can I have a few days to think about it?" Caroline asked, biting her lip hard to keep from saying yes.

"Of course, I'll look forward to hearing from you on Tuesday," Hanna said.

"Tuesday," Caroline said as the call disconnected.

"What's Tuesday?" Sam asked, making Caroline jump.

She pressed the phone to her chest. "What?"

"Tuesday. You said it as you were getting off the phone," Sam said, his brows drawing together. "Everything okay? You know you can talk to me."

"Everything is fine." More than fine. She walked to the far counter, grabbing a box of saltines. "I forgot to get the crackers."

Chapter Eleven

Sam helped Rob load the third Christmas tree onto the back of Sam's truck. Rob stomped his feet and rubbed his hands together. "How's Bryson? You mentioned to Kelly that he wasn't feeling well."

"Severe cold. Poor kid has an awful bark in his chest. Mom thought it might be croup, but Doctor Philips assured her it's a deep chest cold." Sam leaned against the truck. "We'll be sitting out for Thanksgiving dinner this year."

"That's too bad." Rob clasped him on the shoulder as a compact sedan pulled into the parking lot. "Kelly and I will keep him in our prayers. She'll be disappointed not to see you, but I almost figured you might go elsewhere."

"Elsewhere?" Sam shoved away from the truck, recognizing Caroline's car.

Rob tilted his head toward Caroline's car. "You didn't get an invitation elsewhere?"

"Would it matter if I did?" Sam moved toward Caroline's car as she parked. "No one dresses a turkey like Kelly."

Rob walked with him to the car. "That's my wife, best cook in town."

Sam wouldn't argue. Kelly owned and ran the diner in town.

She closed for the holidays. For the past several years, Sam and Bryson had places at the Harrison table.

"Hey, Rob!" Caroline waved as she got out of the car.

Rob picked up his pace. "You're right on time."

Caroline adjusted the red scarf around her neck as she walked to the back of the car. "Dad doesn't like to be kept waiting. Last I heard, Mom had to hide a few of those pies we made so there would be enough for Sunday."

"I'm looking forward to having a slice. Did you help make them, or were you too busy with the wreaths?"

"You don't want me making pies." Caroline lifted the back of her trunk. "They sent me on errands and left me with dish duty. Although, I got a few of these done. Aunt Mar made the bows."

Rob whistled. "You have more? These might not last."

"You flatter me, but we'll be lucky if they sell. I didn't have a lot of time, so they're mostly plain."

Sam stepped close to pull out a few of the pine wreaths. "Sometimes less is more."

Caroline grabbed several swags with baler twine and red bows. Rob took them from her. "I made cards too, hoping people would see the floral shop is open again this season."

"I'll get to those shelves by the weekend," Sam said.

"Dad offered to help. I know you're busy, and I shouldn't have asked." Caroline scooped up several long swags, and Rob shut the trunk. "I'll show you where to hang these. I made space in the barn."

The barn Rob referred to was a small barn with a porch. The side doors slid open, allowing customers to come in and browse some trees already cut and leaning together in the middle. A hot chocolate stand sat in one corner with the addition of coffee and tea. The entire back wall had pegs he and Rob installed earlier that morning to prepare for Caroline's wreaths and swags.

"Thank you, Rob. I know Aunt Marge really appreciates this," Caroline said as they approached the wall. Rob placed wreaths on the wall and then heard another vehicle. "I'll take those," Sam offered.

"Caroline's probably better at arranging them, anyway." Rob dumped the extras on Sam. "That's probably Luke bringing by the tree stands he made to restock."

"Luke Meyers?" Caroline asked.

"Yep." Sam reached up and placed a wreath on a peg. Rob walked off, heading back outside. "You should go out and say hello."

"I didn't know he was living back home again."

"He came back after his dad passed. His mom's at the retirement home, and Luke's running the salvage yard. His wife Bridget likes to repurpose stuff and sells it. They're a perfect pair. If she's not with him, you'll probably meet her on Sunday. You're coming to the church dinner after the tree lighting, right?"

"I told Aunt Marge I would take her."

Sam reached over her and hung up another swag.

"How is Bryson?"

"Chest cold."

Caroline went silent, hanging swags and tilting wreaths for display.

"Poor kid. Turkey dinner won't be as exciting for him."

"Mom never cooks. Dad likes it on his own. He used to cook when I was younger."

Caroline hung another swag, her hair slipping out from her scarf. He resisted the urge to reach over and slide it between his fingers.

She tilted her head, looking at the wreath. "You're welcome to come have dinner with us. It's a bit earlier than most people eat. Dad doesn't have the patience to wait for pie. Mom won't let him have any until after turkey."

"Will your sisters be there?"

Caroline sighed.

"I'm sure they enjoy having you home."

"But you're going to decline my offer."

"I need to stay home with Bry. I don't want to take him out anywhere until he's feeling better." Sam put up the last swag and grinned at her. "There. All done."

"Thanks, Sam." Caroline stepped back, glancing at their work. Her face beamed infectiously. Sam leaned against her, shoulder to shoulder. "I'll bring you more pine branches in a few days. I usually deliver Marge's trees to her and help set them up."

"That's very kind of you." Caroline stared at the wreaths ahead.

Sam watched her, sliding his hands back into his pockets. "Give me a day or two, and I'll get those shelves done for you. Once Bry's feeling better, I can bring him with me."

"Dad and I can get the shelves done, Sam. Don't worry about it. Take care of Bryson. He needs you most." Caroline tucked her hands in her pockets and shivered. "I need to go or else my sisters will call out the cavalry to find me."

"You mean they haven't put a tracker on you?" Sam teased, trying to lighten the mood. He wanted Caroline to smile again.

"They would if they could. I'm smart enough to not let them get hold of my phone." She pulled it out of her pocket and wiggled it in front of him.

"I'm glad you're back," Sam said, slipping for a moment and retracting his words. "What I mean is, I'm sure your family appreciates having you home. Have you thought about staying? I'm sure Marge would gladly accept help in the flower shop and the bed-and-breakfast."

"I am not sure. I got a job offer." She turned toward him. "If I take it, I'd be back at the university again, and I could return to my old life," her voice lowered. She glanced around. "Then I wouldn't be lying to my family anymore, and they wouldn't know I lost my job."

"Is that what you want?" Sam rubbed the heel of his hand against his chest to ease the sensation there. "To go back? He's still there, isn't he? Your ex?"

Caroline paled, and Sam wished he could give himself a good swift kick for causing her distress. "I didn't mean to pry."

"No." Caroline took a deep breath, her gaze going to her furry-rimmed boots. "Josh attends the university. It's why he wanted me to work there. All while we were married, he got free tuition."

"Wow," Sam said. What a jerk!

"Yeah," Caroline agreed. "Josh loves to learn. He wants to teach one day, except I don't think he'll ever give up being a student."

"How does that make you feel?"

Caroline pushed back a strand of hair inching across her cheek. "At first, I let it go. I knew he wanted to get his doctorate and teach at the college level. He's smart. Sometimes too smart. But then I realized all the things he told me were lies. Maybe deep down he wanted those things, but his agenda didn't have room for me or children until further down the road. I don't want to be middle-aged with toddlers. And yet"—she shrugged—"Here I am."

"I'm sorry." Sam didn't know what else to say. This wasn't the version Janelle had given him. "I take it your sisters don't know all this?"

"My family knows Josh was only using me to support his endeavors. My father never liked him and his 'city slicker' ways."

"You met him at the university?" Sam couldn't help asking.

"Yep, and I should have known then, but love blinded me."

"You still love him?"

"Do you still love Bryson's mother?" she countered.

"Maybe. I thought I did." Sam spoke the truth. Megan fascinated him. She introduced him to a world beyond the small town he always knew. He'd fallen deep into the exploration of all the things his parents told him not to do. "I met Megan my second year at the academy. She worked at this convenience store on the corner. It took me a few months before I got the nerve to ask her out."

"You didn't marry?" Caroline bit her lip.

He cleared his throat and looked away. "No. She wouldn't have me. Turns out I wasn't the only man in her life."

Caroline gasped. "Oh, Sam. I'm sorry."

"I got Bryson. That's all that counts."

"You're blessed to have a son." She glanced at her phone, checking the time. He took a step toward her, and she turned, taking the motion as a signal to leave.

"Perhaps one day, you'll have children, too."

"Who knows what plans God has in store for us, right?" Caroline walked out of the barn with Sam following.

"Hey, Sam, give us a hand, will you?" Rob shouted. He and Luke were carrying handfuls of tree stands.

"Hey, Caroline." Luke lifted his chin since his hands were full. "I heard you were back. How long you in for?"

Sam held his breath as he waited for her answer.

"I'm not sure," Caroline said, sending a whoosh of relief through him. "It's good to see you, Luke. I've got to get going. Hopefully, I'll see you later." She waved and was off.

Sam went to the truck, gathered the last of the tree stands, and followed Luke and Rob into the barn. "Well?" Rob asked, his brows wiggling.

"What?" Sam put down the tree stands.

Rob looked at Luke and said, "See? I told you so."

Luke crossed his arms. He stared at Sam a moment, then nodded. "Yep. I think you're right."

Sam growled. "You two going to tell me what you're talking about?"

Luke walked past him, saying as he went, "You and Caroline. Now that she's back, maybe you'll ask her out this time."

"I wouldn't wait too long," Rob said.

"She's not planning on staying." Sam listened for the sounds of her car pulling out of the lot.

"Not if you don't show her what she's got to stay for."

"She's got a job in the city," Sam said.

"She's got plenty to do here. Kelly said Janelle told her that Brenda is making her a website to get the floral shop in the black again."

Sam bit back his thoughts. He wouldn't break Caroline's confidence. What if Caroline decided not to take the job and go back? Could he show her by staying here he could offer her everything she wanted?

Chapter Twelve

Sam wasn't the only one Caroline confided in about her job situation. She told Aunt Marge, the one person she could count on to keep her secrets. She'd been so surprised by how easy talking to Sam seemed. They'd grown apart the older they'd gotten. She remembered Sam had eyes for Fara Brady and asked her to the prom their senior year. That had been a long time ago, and like the counselor she saw in the first few months of her dissolved marriage, she needed to learn to let go. It did no good to dwell on what couldn't be changed.

She sat through Thanksgiving dinner with her family. Dad at the head of the table and her mother at the other. She and her sisters sat on one side. Janelle's husband, Ben, sat across from her with Aunt Marge and Aunt Maeve. Ben talked football with their father as they retired to watch the game on television.

Caroline helped clean up, washing the dishes as Brenda transferred the leftovers into containers for heating later. Janelle cut the pie and checked on the children, Caroline's nephews, Liam and Benny, had crawled on the couch. Janelle made them plates and sat them at the coffee table while the adults ate. Benny sat with his iPad playing games appropriate for a six-year-old, while Liam crawled on Ben's lap and nestled in to watch football.

"Mom's going to watch them while we go tonight," Janelle said, finishing distributing the pie.

"I'm meeting friends," Brenda said. "Don't forget, Carrie, we need to tweak the website. I need some more photos."

Her sisters had reverted to calling her by Dad's nickname. She'd had them trained after she left to stop calling her by her childhood name. It made her feel small and immature, but the day Sam had said it sent an entirely different feeling inside her. Josh always called her by her proper name.

"Caroline, that means you'll have to stay and help Mom with the boys," Janelle said.

"She can't," Aunt Mar came into the kitchen. "We have guests at the house, and Caroline is helping me with keeping the rooms serviced. We will need to get back soon; I like to have warm beverages available. Some of them will have gone to the tree farm before they leave in the morning. We have several staying for a few more days to see the tree lighting."

"Then, Brenda, I guess it's on you," Janelle said.

"Mom can handle it," Brenda said. "She raised us, Janelle. Otherwise, you'll have to switch plans."

Caroline suppressed a smile. Sometimes her sisters surprised her.

"We should get going soon," Aunt Mar said.

"You should take some food." Mom walked into the kitchen with an empty plate. She would expect it washed and put away immediately.

"Good idea," Caroline said, thinking of Sam. She'd make him a plate and take it to him. No one should be without a good meal on Thanksgiving. A flutter erupted in her stomach with thoughts of him. She'd only been home less than a week. Having feelings for Sam both frightened and excited her. Could it go anywhere?

Not if she left Hidden Hills and went back to the university. The decision weighed on her. Going back to the university meant the prospect of seeing Josh again. Did she want that? Did she want to go back to that type of job?

Brenda had spent hours setting up the website. Despite the lack of photos, she'd done a wonderful job. Caroline had set up a social media account, taking videos as she created the wreaths. Not only could people watch coming into the shop, they'd be able to watch online. Those thoughts warmed her. Staying and spending time with Sam gave her this giddy feeling she didn't know if she wanted to feel for anyone again.

"Won't Duke need to go out soon?" Aunt Mar asked, moving along with their departure. Caroline saw the exhaustion on Aunt Mar's face. As soon as they got back, Aunt Mar would take a nap. She wore a dark green shawl and her big, hooped gold earrings. Her slacks were black, and Aunt Mar went nowhere unless she dressed for the occasion. While Aunt Mar slipped on her shoes and gathered her coat, Caroline headed for the kitchen.

In a matter of minutes, she had two plates of food wrapped and ready to go.

"Running off again?" Dorothy asked. "Maeve and I were about to play a game of cards."

"Duke will need to go out. Aunt Mar has guests," Caroline explained.

"You understand, don't you?" Aunt Mar said. "We all have our families and livelihood to tend."

Caroline's mother scowled. "We're going shopping tomorrow. Be here early."

"She can't," Aunt Mar interjected. "We've got the shop to run."

"It's not open? Janelle said it's still all torn apart and Paul hasn't come over to help build the shelves."

"We don't need shelves to open and take orders. Thanks to Brenda's website, Caroline here will soon be in business online and we need to prepare," Aunt Mar said.

Once Caroline settled Aunt Mar into her car and they started the drive back to the bed-and-breakfast, Aunt Mar said, "You didn't want to go shopping, did you?"

"No," Caroline said, more relieved than disappointed. "Is it bad I'd rather spend the day working in the shop than dealing with... them?"

Aunt Mar clutched the plates of food on her lap. "Some families are more complicated than others. Feel fortunate you have one."

"You're right."

Sam and Bryson came to mind. Sam had his parents, and Bryson had Sam. It didn't make her think any less of them, much the opposite. How very much she'd like to have a son like Bryson.

Pulling into the driveway, Caroline helped Aunt Marge into the house, but as Caroline went to step through, hearing Duke's bark, Marge stopped her. Holding out one of the covered plates of food, she said, "I believe there is one more place you need to go today."

Glancing down at the plates of food, then back up at Aunt Mar, Caroline's hands trembled.

"It's food, Carrie, not a rabid raccoon."

Caroline laughed. "I know what you're up to."

"Well?"

"I need to let Duke out." She could see him prancing behind Aunt Marge.

"Leave the doggy business to me."

Caroline glanced over at Duke, who woofed softly. "Are you sure?"

"I may be old, but I can handle a dog. Duke and I have become quite good friends, haven't we?" At the sound of his name, Duke came up beside Aunt Mar, and she patted him on the head.

"Okay, I won't be long."

"Take all the time you need," Aunt Mar said, shooing her off.

Back in her car, Caroline pulled out her phone. She resisted the temptation to text Sam. Once she texted him, she would want to do it often.

Sam lived with his parents in the same white house down the road between her parents and the pig farm. In less than twenty minutes, she had spotted his truck parked at the house. Two other vehicles sat in the driveway, and Caroline pulled off to the side of the road.

Her heart hammering, she glanced at the plates of food on the seat beside her. "You can do this, Caroline," she coached herself. "Like Aunt Mar said, it's just food."

Taking the plates of food before she could change her mind, Caroline headed to the front door. The plates radiated heat and warmed her icy fingers. In her haste, she'd forgone putting on gloves.

Hitting the doorbell, she sucked in a breath and waited. Reaching up, she pushed her hair away from her eyes. She'd pulled it back in a twist for dinner at her parents'. Soon the sky would darken as the evening grew into night. Caroline wasn't a fan of driving at night. She shifted from one foot to another. About to knock this time, the door opened.

A woman answered the door. Her honey blond hair was pulled back in a ponytail, and her brown sweater dress hung to her knees. "Oh my gosh, Caroline!"

When Caroline didn't respond, the woman said, "Sonya. I'm Sonya Willsie. Markle now, but my husband, Jake, passed a few years ago. What are you doing here? It's so good to see you! I heard you were in visiting."

Caroline's spirits fell. "I came to drop off some food for Sam since Bryson wasn't feeling well."

"You heard about that?" Sonya leaned in the doorway, blocking the entrance. "Poor little guy. He hangs out with my son, Jimmy. The two of them are as close as brothers. When Jimmy heard Bryson couldn't come to Thanksgiving dinner, he asked if we could bring it to Bryson. Of course, I didn't want Sam and his dad to be left out, so we came over earlier this morning to cook. Gladys felt so bad she got called in to work today."

"That was very kind of you."

"And you." Sonya grabbed the food plates from her hands. "I'll put these in the fridge for them for later. With all I have here plus this"—she raised the plates—"Gladys won't have to cook for the entire weekend."

"Is Sam here?" Without the plates to warm her hands, she shoved them in her pockets.

"He's upstairs with the boys. They're playing video games. I was about to call them for dinner. I hope you don't mind. I need to get things on the table." Sonya smiled, lifting the plates. "Thanks again for this. I'll let Sam know you were thinking of him."

"Great," Caroline said, gritting her teeth against the cold.

The door shut, leaving her standing on the porch, her insides going as cold as the frost forming on her lashes.

Spinning around on her heel, she marched back to her car. Turning on the heat, she didn't spare another moment lingering at Sam's house. She should have taken the hint when he said he wanted to be her friend.

For a moment, she'd allowed her emotions to get the best of her. Tears streaked down her cheeks. Her decision was made. She couldn't stay in Hidden Hills.

Chapter Thirteen

SOMETHING HAD CHANGED SINCE THANKSGIVING. SAM showed up at Marge's to work on the shop and found it painted cream with white lights draped across the ceiling. Ladder shelves, the kind purchased from a retail store, sat with flower displays in the center of the room. A makeshift counter with supplies in plastic drawers sat like an island near the back, and on the long inner wall, two coolers awaited fresh flowers.

She'd placed a small counter-height bookcase open on both sides with check-out supplies and her card reader. He found everything he needed to work on the shelves, opening the picture on his phone as a reminder of what Caroline wanted.

He'd texted her several times over the past few days. Unease crept up his spine, thinking she left and went back to the city.

"Oh, Sam," Marge said, stepping into the floral shop. "Doesn't this place look wonderful?"

"It does," he agreed.

"It'll look so beautiful once you've created the shelves. Caroline has outdone herself, even if Janelle had a few insights for her. I could have never imagined it looking this lovely." Marge clasped her hands together.

"Speaking of Caroline. Is she around?" Sam asked.

Marge pulled her shawl closer around her. "She left yesterday for Louisville, but she should be back later today."

"She went back to Louisville?"

"She needed to take care of a matter at the university. Since she was going that far, she promised to stop and bring some fresh flowers to fill the coolers again. It will be lovely to have some poinsettias giving this place a pop of Christmas cheer."

"It will indeed." Sam set down his tools near the wood planks by the work counter. "You said she went to the university?"

Marge stared at him a long moment. "Yes, that's what I said. I thought you might have known. I take it you and her didn't talk about future schedules when she dropped off the plates of food on Thanksgiving."

Sam's forehead creased.

"You didn't know she stopped by?" Marge tsked.

"No. Sonya stopped by with Jimmy, and we had Thanksgiving dinner with my parents before I headed over to the tree farm to help Rob. Which reminds me, Rob said to tell Caroline they need more wreaths. I texted her, but she hasn't responded."

"I'm sure she will. Reception here can be spotty at times, as you know." Marge stepped further into the shop. "Your friendship means a lot to her. I want you to know that."

Sam shed his jacket. Caroline or no Caroline, he would build her shelves like he said he would. A gnawing in his gut chided him for not asking Caroline out. A situation he planned to rectify when he saw her again. *If* he saw her again. The gnawing in his gut increased. Marge would tell him if she knew about Caroline's job situation, wouldn't she?

Sam scratched the growth on his chin. He let his beard grow in for the winter months.

"Any idea when she'll return?"

"Before dinner."

"I didn't see her on Sunday. I hoped to run into her at the tree lighting."

"She missed it to stay here. We still have a couple of guests, and I don't like to leave the house empty when I have people staying. Caroline offered to stay so I could see the lights with Jimmy."

"Marge," Sam hated to ask, feeling like a wet-behind-the-ears teenager.

She beat him to it. "Have you told her how you feel?"

"She's only been back for a little over a week." He couldn't feel this way about someone this fast and make it last, could he? He made that mistake with Megan.

"And if you don't let her know your intentions, she won't be here past Christmas," Marge said.

"You know about the job offer?" Marge frowned, and Sam ran his hands through his hair. "You didn't know."

"I may be old, but I raised two boys. I'm not entirely oblivious. Does this job include returning to Louisville?"

"The university offered her a new position. I guess it's in a different department. She'd start in a few weeks."

"She told you this?"

Sam nodded, swallowing hard.

"Then my niece trusts you. That's saying something." Marge glanced around the shop. "I hoped she'd stay and take over the place. I've been praying for her ever since Josh betrayed her. To know she trusted you enough to confide anything gives me hope."

It made Sam feel worse.

"I'm headed into the kitchen to bake some cookies for later. I'll turn on the coffee pot if you want a cup as you work."

"Thanks, Marge."

"No." Marge waved her hand. "Thank you, Sam."

"I don't understand. What for?"

Slowly, Marge smiled, the joy of it lighting up her eyes. "For the shelves. For caring about Caroline. And to prove this old woman hasn't lost her marbles yet."

Sam went to work on the shelves for Caroline. He pulled out his phone, texting her one more time.

The shop looks great.

A moment later, three dots appeared. He waited.

Then the dots disappeared, and she left him without a reply again. His fingers smoothed over the screen of his phone. Would she respond if he asked her to have lunch with him at the diner one day this week?

Instead, he texted her, *Be safe driving home. I look forward to seeing you and hearing about your trip.*

He paused before hitting send. Should he tell her he knew about the university? OR that he told Marge about the job switch? Would telling her he wanted her to stay, or he missed her these past few days seem to be attached and scare her?

It scared him.

He closed his eyes, hitting the send button in the process and praying to God Caroline would stay. As selfish as it might seem, he wanted more time to spend with her. He wasn't sure about the rest of the family, but he was certain Marge felt the same way and would approve.

Then he remembered the food, the plates Marge said she brought him on Thanksgiving. He texted Sonya.

> Did Carrie stop by on Thanksgiving? Drop off food?

> Who's Carrie?

> Caroline

> ..... Oh. Yeah. I must have forgotten to tell you.

> Thanks

> Anytime :)

Chapter Fourteen

CAROLINE SAT IN HER CAR LOOKING AT THE administrative building of the university. Beside her on the seat lay an envelope with all the requested material to start her new job. A swirl of emotions caused her to keep her grip on the steering wheel. She watched people with their heads ducked and backpacks walk briskly down the sidewalks, headed for classroom buildings. She didn't envy them. Caroline never enjoyed taking classes but had done it to have the knowledge she needed to one day own her own business. A business that would allow her to stay home and raise a family. Seeing the university made her think of Josh.

Bitterness rose and burned in her chest. For a moment, she thought she might be sick. Beside her, the ding of a message caught her attention.

> Website working. 1st sale!

Phone in hand and papers in the other, it took Caroline less than fifteen minutes to meet with Hanna from HR. Brenda's message brought little relief.

Caroline should have known before she even walked back out

of the building her ex-husband would call her. She ignored the sound.

The rest of her day was spent driving and visiting the greenhouse where Aunt Marge had called in an order of floral supplies. It included fresh cuts for creating centerpieces and other requests from the residents of Hidden Hills.

By the time she picked up the order, browsed, and added a few selections of her own, it was dark when she pulled in front near the porch to carry in the supplies. As she opened the back door, she spotted Sam coming down the stairs. Bryson raced past him. "Caroline! Caroline!"

"Hey, you." She pushed down the flood of emotions. "I take it you're feeling better?"

"Bry, you need to grab your coat. Back in the house!" Sam said sternly.

Bryson made a face.

"You should listen to your father. You don't want to get sick again."

"If I do, will you make me some of your mom's soup?"

"Of course."

Bryson did a fist pump and took off for the stairs again. Caroline turned, pulling out a Styrofoam cooler.

"Here, let me help you." Sam held out his arms. While the weather had warmed up to almost forty degrees in the day, the chill of the wind brushed against Caroline's cheeks and made her shiver. She gave Sam the cooler as she grabbed the other.

He had to have raced by the time she turned around again. He appeared empty-handed. "Is there more?" He took that one from her, too.

"Some things in the trunk." She shut the back door of her sedan. Popping the trunk, she grabbed a few boxes. Sam waited for her to lead the way as she went up the stairs inside the shop. Caroline paused, spotting the new wood shelves. "Sam," she breathed.

"I take it you like them?"

"They're just like the picture." She sat the cooler of flowers beside the other one on the workbench.

"Not exactly. They still need to be stained."

"I can do that."

"I'm sure you can." He sat the boxes in his arms on the floor. "Stay here where it's warm. I'll grab the rest."

"You don't have to do that," she protested.

He grinned that heart-melting smile that made her all gooey inside. "I want to."

How would this friendship thing work if she got all warm inside when he came around her?

"Marge made hot chocolate and cookies. You want some?" Bryson grinned from the open doors between the shop and the house.

"Absolutely." Caroline tried to shake off these feelings she got around Sam. He had a girlfriend, and she had no place as anything more than a friend in his life.

"But first, I need to get these flowers taken care of before they wilt and they're not any good to us."

"I can help." Bryson came into the shop wearing a dark hoodie and matching socks. She could appreciate Sam telling him to get back inside. Shivering, she reached for the first container of flowers.

"Are you cold?" Bryson asked.

"A little," Caroline confessed, deciding to keep her jacket on for a while, despite the warmth in the room. "I'd better go get you some hot chocolate. You don't want to get a cold. It sucks." Bryson took off toward the kitchen.

"Wait, have you seen Duke?" she asked.

"Kitchen," Bryson called, disappearing into the house.

Caroline pulled out flowers and arranged them in the correct pails and put them in water in the tall glass door coolers.

Sam came back, shutting the door and setting the last of the supplies down. "If you tell me where these go, I can help."

"The small boxes go over by the register. I got some pretty

bags, tags, and bows. The medium ones and large ones are ribbon, containers, and silk flowers. They can go over by the workbench here. I'll sort it later."

Bryson ducked his head in, Duke beside him. "Mar is making the hot chocolate. It'll be a few minutes."

"Sounds great." Caroline reached for a bundle of red roses.

"You know," Bryson said, walking up to her. "I don't get it. Why do you put flowers in a cooler? Won't they die?"

"Nope." Caroline took the bunch of white roses next. "It helps prolong their life once they've been cut. If it's too hot, they'll wilt faster."

"Really?" Bryson crossed his arms, looking as if he didn't believe her.

"Really." Sam reached in and pulled out a white blossomed flower. He turned it, looking oddly at it, and she took it from his hands. "Christmas rose."

"We have these around here?"

"For the holiday. Aunt Mar is going to show me how to make some centerpieces for the craft bazaar at the church next Saturday."

"I'm glad you're here, Carrie."

Her heart tripped at the sound of her name. She wanted to hear him say it again. Silly as it seemed, she wanted to hear his voice every day.

"What did I say? And don't tell me it's nothing."

She finished storing the live flowers for later. "I can't tell you, Sam." It would ruin the friendship they'd been building.

"You can tell me anything. I'm not going anywhere, I swear." He put his hand up like a boy scout.

She pulled his fingers down, and he grasped hers, holding her fingers captive, sending tickles of awareness up her arm. Tiny goosebumps prickled beneath her jacket. She loathed having to take it off, not wanting him to take her reaction the wrong way.

"I don't know how long I'll be here." She told him the truth. Hanna's offer was still on the table from the university.

Sam held on, his fingers warm against her cool skin. "Then come to the tree lighting with Bryson and me in the park Friday night. You'll be here then, won't you?"

"What about your girlfriend?"

He jerked back as if her words were a slap in the face. "Girlfriend?" He truly appeared dumb-struck. Then, as if a light turned on inside his brain, his lips parted in acknowledgment. She resisted the urge once more to reach out and touch the scruff forming against his jaw. In some rough-mannered way, she found his growing beard fascinating.

Josh would have never allowed more than a five o'clock shadow on his face. She shook the image of her ex-husband out of her head. He couldn't hold back her future anymore.

"You mean Sonya?" Sam leaned forward. "She's not my girlfriend. Her son Jimmy plays sometimes with Bry. She works at the bank with Lisa Shaw, Luke's sister."

"She was at your house on Thanksgiving and answered the door when I dropped off the food. I shouldn't have assumed." She lowered her gaze to where his fingers entrapped hers, warmth radiating into her palm.

"We usually get together at Rob and Kelly's. When she heard about Bry not feeling well, she came over to return the favor," he explained. "When her son, Jimmy, got burned, Luke went to the hospital and some of us pitched in to help. Sonya's a widow."

"That's awful." More than awful. None of these things entitled her to know someone else's business. "You don't have to tell me any more."

"There are a lot of things you've missed while you were away," Sam said.

"I'm sure Janelle would have informed me of most of them, but I tried to avoid the gossip the times she or my mom would call. They always ended with a plea or demand I come home where I belong."

"I can't say I don't disagree with that." Sam slipped his fingers under her hand, gently stroking her palm. "What do you say? Will you go to the tree lighting with us?"

"I don't know if that's a good idea. What will Bryson think?"

"Why don't you ask him?" Sam glanced over his shoulder. "What do you say, Bry? Want Caroline to come to the tree lighting ceremony with us on Friday?"

"Yes! You have to come! Please? Please?" Bryson jumped up and down.

"Saturday is the craft bazaar at the church."

"We can help you," Bryson said.

How could she resist an offer like that? "Okay, you got yourself a deal."

Chapter Fifteen

Sam worked at the pig farm in the mornings, did odd jobs in the afternoons, and worked at the tree farm in the evenings. Twice during the week, he stopped by the bed-and-breakfast to find Caroline and Marge in the shop, working on some flower creation or another.

He brought lunch one day from the diner, treating both Caroline and Marge to the daily special of macaroni and cheese with a meatloaf sandwich. The next time he came, he planned to stain the shelves, but Caroline beat him to it.

As he walked inside the shop, he took a moment to look around. There were centerpieces gracing the shelves. According to Rob, he sold a steady amount of wreaths with red bows. Enough wreaths. Sam had another stack of pine branches on the back of his truck for Caroline. He'd picked a few pinecones for her as a surprise.

The closer they came to Friday, the more Sam looked forward to their date. He'd never seen his son more excited to go to a Christmas tree lighting in his life.

He found Caroline taking photos and humming. Watching her work, he stayed back quiet, returning to her laptop and typing something. Duke stretched from the dog bed near her chair. The

Golden Retriever padded across the shop and sat down in front of him.

"It's nice to see you, too." Sam reached down to run his hand over the dog's head.

"Sam!" Caroline shot to her feet. "What are you doing here? It's not Friday."

He grinned, holding out a bag. "Cookies from Johnson's Bakery."

"Why do I have a feeling I'm going to see you every day?" She got up and walked around the work table.

"I come through town a lot. Can you blame a man for wanting to stop in and say hello?"

She tilted her head, onto his tactics, and reached for the bag. Yanking it back, he held it slightly out of reach. "You can only have this if you have some coffee to go with them."

She wagged her finger. "You're a sly one, but it so happens that Aunt Mar went in to make tea a little while ago. I think we can arrange something."

"Do you still have guests?"

Caroline opened the French doors with glass panes leading into the house. "Not until Friday. There are a few people coming in for the tree lighting and the craft bazaar. Regulars, I'm told."

"Is Scott coming in this year for the holidays?"

Caroline frowned. "Aunt Mar hadn't mentioned it. I don't think he's come home in years."

"It's been hard on her." Sam jutted his chin toward the inside of the house. "I don't know what I would do not seeing Bry every day. I can't imagine not seeing him for years."

"Even as an adult?" Caroline mused.

"Bryson will always be my son, no matter his age. I want to be a part of his life always. Marge must miss her son, seeing he's the only family left."

"She has my mom and Aunt Maeve."

"It's hardly the same, don't you think?"

Caroline frowned, deep in thought. "I suppose."

"Ask your mother, she probably will tell you the same."

Caroline snorted, reached out, and grabbed the bag before he could stop her. "Hey, give those back."

She jumped away from him, dangling the bag in front of her. "Oh, they're mine now."

Sam growled playfully. "We'll see about that."

Caroline's eyes got huge. She raced off for the kitchen, Duke barking and joining the chase. Sam dashed around the couch inside the living room while Caroline ran to the other side.

She wore her hair up in a messy bun and wore a cute sweater with snowmen and snowflakes who danced in the motion of her movements. She laughed as he came around the couch—her heading for the kitchen, and him trying to get to the doorway first.

He hooked her around the waist, pulling her back against him. The bag of cookies dangled from her outstretched hand.

"You'd best give me those cookies, woman. I know your mother taught you to share."

"Well, if you put it that way..." Caroline giggled as she turned in his arms. Suddenly, her expression changed. Sam's arms went around her. The bag of cookies crinkled between them. Several strands of her dark hair curled around her face. He leaned in close, his breath warming her ear. "I know something you don't know."

She shivered at his near-touch. He had her where he wanted her, his gaze on those lips a fraction of an inch away. Her breath came in quick little pants. Then suddenly, he snatched the bag between them and beat her to the kitchen.

A moment later, she appeared, her eyes blazing with challenge. He laughed, holding out a cookie toward her. Marge sat at the table, sipping her tea and looking amused.

Caroline quirked a brow, reaching for the offered confection. Before she could grasp it, he had it in his mouth and took a bite.

Caroline gasped. "Rude."

"They're Johnson Bakery cookies." Sam grinned, loving the shocked expression on Caroline's face. "Careful, you wouldn't want your face to freeze like that," he taunted, using one of Bry's favorite expressions.

"Aunt Mar, did you see what he did?" She turned to her aunt for support.

Mar eased herself up from the table. Picking up her tea, she walked toward the dining room. "I'm too old to get in the middle of this, but I will say once you've had a cookie from Johnson's, you'd do the same thing." Glancing at Sam, she shook her head. "Greed is a sin."

The rest of the cookie dropped out of his mouth, and Caroline's frown turned into a laughing smile, her eyes twinkling with trouble to come.

Chapter Sixteen

CAROLINE OPENED THE SHOP EARLY. PRIDE SWELLING inside her, she sat at the counter making more pine swags for the bazaar on Saturday. Sam texted her twice, and she paused at the emojis he sent her—a silly face and a Christmas tree. Needing a break, she headed for the kitchen. Going through the French doors leading into the house, she spied Duke lying on a blanket on the couch. Pausing, she tilted her head, "Hey boy. Want a treat?"

He looked at her with those droopy brown eyes, and she sighed. "I miss him, too." She walked over and patted him on the head. "We'll see him tonight." Duke raised his head and woofed softly.

Giving him a good scratch behind the ears, she promised to take him along with her that evening for the tree lighting in the park.

Inside the kitchen, Aunt Mar worked. The scent of cinnamon and sugar was a pleasant welcome. "More cookies?" she asked, coming in and spotting a woman by the counter with flour on her cheek and hands.

"Oh, there you are!" Aunt Marge turned from taking fresh

cookies out of the oven. "I was just telling Bridget we might have to come pull you out of the shop."

"You'd only had to open the door to let this wonderful scent in." Caroline inhaled. "Why didn't you tell me you were baking? I could have helped."

"You are busy with the shop." Aunt Marge placed the cookie tray down and started transferring hot snickerdoodles onto the cooling rack.

"It looks great," the woman beside Aunt Marge said, thrusting out her head. "I'm Bridget."

A moment of confusion must have flittered on her face, for as she took the woman's hand, Marge said, "Luke's wife. Bridget stayed here at the house with me while she and Luke were dating."

"Congratulations," Caroline said, as the handshake became a hug. She tensed, and Bridget drew away.

"I'm sorry. I should have asked if you were a hugger. After staying with Marge for so long, it made me feel like we're family."

And Caroline believed the sincerity in her voice. Aunt Marge had a way of bringing people in and making them feel at home. If she would admit it, she always loved that about her aunt. She came here often trying to escape her family, to have her own space, and Aunt Marge always seemed to understand and know what she needed.

Bridget dusted off her hands in her apron. "I hope you don't mind. I brought you a few things I thought you could use for in the shop. You can do with them whatever you'd like." Bridget moved inside the dining room and Caroline followed. She wore a flannel shirt, too big in the shoulders, and Caroline guessed it belonged to Luke. Bridget wore her hair drawn back, a cascade of warmth flowing from her. "Luke picked these up somewhere. I meant to bring them over sooner. Little Lizzy helped me clean them up, and we painted them. I thought they'd look nice in the windows out front here of the B&B. You can put battery or electric candles in where the votives are and change out the flowers for the different seasons." Bridget held up several sconces, all painted a shiny gold. "These are perfect." Caroline accepted them from Bridget. "Can I pay you for them?"

"After all the time Marge let me stay here? Are you kidding?" Bridget slid a box full of more of them toward Caroline. "If no one has told you, Luke likes to go around picking up junk, and I like to repurpose it. We've got a shop of our own at the farm. I transformed the milk house into our own little place."

"I'll have to check it out sometime."

"Please do. I'll have items at the bazaar."

"Me too." Caroline beamed, feeling at ease with Luke's wife.

They spoke for a few more minutes, giving each other ideas for the sconces and then talking shop. It seemed Caroline's sister Brenda was making good on her skills, having helped Bridget with a website, too.

They had cookies and tea in the kitchen before Bridget excused herself to go back to her own shop. While Caroline helped Aunt Marge clean up after the cookie mess, her aunt tried to keep her from doing the dishes. "Sit." Caroline pointed at the chair nearest to Marge there, at the small kitchen table.

"You've done so much already. You've done a wonderful thing in the floral shop. I knew it just needed your special touch."

Caroline pressed her lips together for a moment, her heart and her head at war. She'd always been able to tell Aunt Mar everything, including things she could never share with her mother. Her shoulders sagged as the confession rolled up to the tip of her tongue.

"You're going with Sam to the tree lighting this evening?" Aunt Marge asked with a sigh.

Caroline glanced over her shoulder at her aunt, the lines of fatigue settling in on her face. "Yes, but you're coming as well? The Franchis are here tonight. They will be going out to dinner and attending the lighting before they come back.

"I told Maeve I would keep her company. Your mother offered to pick us up." Aunt Marge closed her eyes for a moment's rest.

"Dad's not going?" Why did this not surprise her? He probably had an excuse to check in on his cows or keep the coal burning for the house to stay warm.

"Your mother said he was helping the Evans today and wouldn't have time to get his own chores done."

Likely excuse, but Caroline kept the thought to herself. "Aunt Mar?"

"I'm glad you and Sam are getting along and spending time together," Aunt Mar said. "That boy of his has taken a liking to you. Child needs more than his grandmother and me in his life."

"I suppose he does." Caroline wiped the last of the dishes. "There's something I've been meaning to talk to you about."

This made her aunt open her eyes. "What's that, dear?"

Caroline took a deep breath and turned. She leaned back against the sink counter. "The university offered me a job.

"And is that what you want? I thought the university left you go.?" Aunt Mar said.

Caroline clasped her hands together. "Due to lack of funding, they cut jobs last semester."

"You were always welcome to come back here sooner."

"Can you imagine if I called home and told mom or any of my sisters?"

"They would have had your father out there packing you up to come home in an instant,"

"I needed time."

"And this was the time." It wasn't a question so much as it was a fact. One that had Aunt Marge beaming. "You are an answer to prayer, Caroline. You know that, don't you?"

"I dare ask who. Aunt Marge. I told you I don't know what I'm doing here. The lease on my apartment ended, and without a job, I had no choice. I put my stuff in storage, not that I had much." She winced, thinking of the meager possessions she'd kept ahold of after the split with Josh. He wouldn't leave, so she'd had to pack what she could and find another place to live. Starting over again was the hardest and best thing she could have done. She could see that now. Walking over and taking a chair across from

Aunt Marge, she let it all spill. The truth of why her marriage fell apart. Her job loss. The offer of the new one. And the decisions she'd made. While she spoke, she looked at her hands.

Aunt Marge covered Caroline's hands with her own. "There is a season for everything, Caroline. That took courage, and I can see why you wouldn't have wanted to tell your mother these things. Dorothy was always a bit of an over-reactor, but she means well. Your mother loves you. We all do."

Caroline swallowed and nodded.

"This is your home. Right here. In this house. In this town." Aunt Marge squeezed her hand. "With Sam and Bryson."

"Aunt Marge..."

"What is your heart telling you?"

Chapter Seventeen

SAM WHISTLED WHILE HE WORKED. THEY SPENT THE morning cutting more trees and tidying the sales shed. Rob hung more of Caroline's wreaths. Sam purchased a few for gifts and sent a few with Luke to the boutiques in Lexington where Luke's wife Bridget sold some of her repurposed pieces on commission.

Outside, Sam stomped his feet to put some feeling back into them. Tanner worked for Rob during the busy season when he wasn't at the feed mill or helping his grandfather, old man Evans, with milking cows on the farm. Tanner rolled back his shoulders, never once complaining about the bitter bite of the winter morning.

As Sam finished wrapping the last bunch of trees for delivery, Tanner filled his thermos with freshly brewed coffee. As they loaded the wrapped trees on the back of Tanner's truck, a forest green Jeep pulled into the lot nearby. "I didn't think Rob had any pick-ups this early." Tanner slammed the tailgate of his truck up.

Sam flexed his hands in his gloves. Tilting his head, he brushed a few pine needles from his coat. "I don't think she's here for a tree."

Tanner raised his brows. "Maybe she's coming to see you? I'm practically a married man."

Sam scowled, then gave Tanner a friendly punch in the arm.

"Just saying." Tanner held up his hands and backed away.

The blonde woman got out of her SUV, opened the back door, and leaned in. "Sam, would you kindly help me with these bags?" Sonya called out.

Sam waved and smiled at her. "Hey, Sonya!" He walked around the truck and helped her bring out three large red bags filled with silver tinseled garland.

She went back to the other side and brought out two shopping bags with red glittery bulbs. "Can you help me with these?" she asked Tanner as he came around his truck, about to get in.

"Sorry, but I got to get these deliveries done and get home before Mariah heads to work. You've got Sam though," Tanner said.

Sonya put on a pretty pout and teased. "Fine. Go make your deliveries, then."

Sam hefted up the bags in his arms. "What's all this?"

Sonya held her own bags close while she used her hip to shut the hatch of her Jeep. "I bought them for the bank, but I got carried away. Kelly mentioned needing some for in the house for their annual Christmas party. I told her I'd drop them off here before going to work. And...." Her cheeks pinked. Sam liked to think it was from the icy chill of the December morning, but the way her eyes watched him, he couldn't be certain. He shifted the bags and slid the door open into the Christmas tree barn. "I was hoping to see you."

"Everything okay?" Sam asked, finding a place to put down the bags without having the silver garland spilling out. He never did care for all the tinsel and glitter people put everywhere for the holidays. White lights, red velvet bows, and pine garlands like the ones Caroline decorated the bed-and-breakfast with from her shop were more to his liking.

"Jimmy is so excited about the tree lighting this evening. We usually go out with Nate and Owen and his family, but I really don't want to be around them this year. It's not that I don't like them, it's just that they remind me so much of Jake. And the way they goof off all the time? It's too much for grown men."

Sam crossed his arms. He could see where she was coming from. Sonya had once been married to Jake Townes, and his brothers were known for getting in trouble. Sam went to her, not long after Jake passed. Single parenthood didn't come easily. They'd both lost someone they'd loved. Neither one of them was certain when they'd move on, but Sam could see the warmth bring color back into her face. Sonya fidgeted with her wool scarf. "Truth is around this time gets hard, you know? Seeing them, and then Jimmy looking like his father and being with his uncles scares me." She sighed, tucking her bags against the others. "If Jake's brothers were here now, I might end up dumping hot chocolate on them. Not that we should do that to people, even if they deserve it," Sonya said.

Sam laughed. He could picture her doing that in his mind for sure.

"Anyway, I thought it might be nice for the two of us. You know? For the boys, really?" She stammered on, correcting herself. "They can watch the lighting together, and you and I don't have to go alone. We can grab hot chocolate and a slice of pecan pie at the diner." Her lips twitched into a smile. "I know it's your favorite. What do you say?"

Sam hesitated for a moment, trying to decide if he should tell Sonya exactly how he felt about spending time with her. The truth was, he had been looking forward to spending some quiet time alone with Caroline after the tree lighting, but now that Sonya had suggested a date with their boys, it suddenly felt like an intrusion. Sam knew he had little time left with Caroline. It wouldn't come very often in the future, and he didn't want to waste it. Not if he could have one last chance to convince her to stay in Hidden Hills.

"That sounds great," Sam felt the need to explain.

Sonya squealed and went to hug him, but Sam put up his arms to stop her. "But..."

He swallowed, looking at her with those suddenly gone-wide eyes. "I already asked Caroline to join us this evening."

"Oh," Sonya said, taking a step back. "I didn't realize you two were dating."

"We're not," Sam jumped to correct her. "We're friends." He grimaced, thinking later he'd need the Lord to forgive him for the lie. They were friends. But deep down, Sam wished they were more.

He could see the hurt spreading in Sonya's eyes.

"You're friends. But you're not dating. And you're taking her to the tree lighting with Bryson."

"I know how that sounds."

"It's really none of my business," Sonya said.

"I want Caroline to stay," Sam blurted.

Sonya tucked her hands in her pockets. "Isn't she running the floral shop at her aunt's place now?"

Sam nodded.

"I heard Marge is moving in with Maeve soon. We all figured the B and B would close like the flower shop. Then Caroline came back and opened it."

"Where did you hear that?" Sam asked.

"I work at the bank." Sonya chuckled. "It's worse than a confessional, the things people tell you when they're making a transaction."

Sam said nothing. A chill went through his bones, sweeping through his gut. Why couldn't people keep their predictions and assumptions to themselves? But they lived in a small town where people liked to spread news. Not all of it always held truth.

"Caroline's in for the holiday. She's just helping her aunt until she goes back," he said.

"She's not going to take over the place and run it?"

"I think her family wants her to do that, but I know she's got a job back in Louisville waiting for her."

"What about the shop?"

"She did it to help Marge. Make her family happy." The more he talked about it, the more sour his stomach turned.

"I see." Sonya glanced away.

Sam rubbed his hand over his face. "Listen, don't say anything alright? It's Caroline's business when she tells her family she's not staying."

Sonya agreed and laid her hand on Sam's arm, a familiar gesture she often did. "I need to head to work, but maybe after Caroline is gone, we can take the boys for that pie and hot chocolate."

"Okay," Sam finally said, smiling at her. "I'd like that, and I'm sure that Jimmy will love watching the town tree lighting with his uncles."

Sonya beamed at him and gave him a quick hug before hurrying out of the Christmas tree barn. Sam watched her go, thinking after all these years, the spark wasn't there for him. Someday, he prayed, God would find someone to love Sonya and her son in Jake's absence.

But perhaps this was better in the long run. Spending time alone with Caroline was something he needed more than anything else right now, and if taking Bryson along made that easier for everyone involved, then it might be worth it after all.

Chapter Eighteen

"This place is awesome!" Bryson exclaimed as he stared out at the town square. The tree was lit up and decorated with thousands of multi-colored lights. A sizable crowd of people had gathered around it and were singing Christmas carols.

Several times Duke barked, trying to sing along. Caroline kept him on a tight leash in case he got any ideas about taking off between them. Bryson patted Duke on the head, and the Golden Retriever woofed again, flicking his tail back and forth.

"It doesn't feel like Christmas until the tree lights up, you know?" Sam said.

A soft smile played on Caroline's lips. She remembered when she was younger, and her father would bring her to the tree lighting with her sisters. Her mother couldn't take standing out in the cold, but as the skies darkened and the tree lit, it filled her heart with an unexpected joy. She looked forward to it every year until she'd left for college. How many other little things that had brought her joy did she forget to have a new life, a better life, away from Hidden Hills?

Sam slid his hand in hers, the heat radiating through her soft knit gloves. "Do you remember the year Kyle pressed his tongue to the light pole?"

"Someone licked a light pole?" Bryson asked, making a face.

"Not a wise move," Caroline agreed. Duke pressed up against her leg, otherwise content to stroll beside them. Several vendors came out during the tree lighting, selling hot chocolate, warm pretzel sticks, roasted nuts, and glow sticks for the kids to run around in the dark.

"Can we get some hot chocolate at the diner before we go?" Bryson shifted from foot to foot. She couldn't blame the kid. The temperatures dropped after the sun went down. That new snow smell teased at the tip of her nose.

"Be back in a few." Sam gave her hand a squeeze, it sent a feeling of warmth to blossom through her chest.

"Come to think of it," Caroline said to Bryson, "I think hot chocolate is a great idea."

"I'm getting cold," Bryson said.

"Stay here with Caroline, okay?" Sam said as he headed across the street toward the still-open diner.

Caroline watched him walk out of sight. Duke kept to her side, and she glanced around, checking for her sisters or one of her aunts. She'd spotted Janelle earlier with her family, before the tree lit. Aunt Marge had been with Aunt Maeve, but Aunt Marge said they wouldn't be staying out in this cold for long. It settled down in her old bones, as Aunt Maeve complained, much like Caroline's mother, Dorothy.

"Hey. Look! It's Jimmy!" Bryson took off, came to a sliding halt, then glanced back. "Is it okay if I go say hi?"

Appreciative of his thoughtfulness, Caroline said, "Stay where I can see you."

The town had placed outdoor heaters in a few spots and extra lighting around the gazebo. Old-fashioned lights lit the way around the square. Beside her, Duke shivered, and she couldn't blame him. "I'm ready to get out of this cold, too."

"Sam said you would be here." Sonya approached. Jimmy and Bryson raced off to the side, chasing each other with snowballs.

"Don't hit anyone with those!" Sonya called before turning back to Caroline. She noticed Sonya wore black fuzzy boots and a black wool jacket with a bright red scarf. Her cherry red lipstick rimmed the edge of the cup she carried. "Where is he, by the way?"

"Sam?" Caroline felt the cold nipping at her cheeks. Soon they'd go numb. "Across the street. Bryson wanted some hot chocolate."

"It's one of the best places in town to get hot chocolate," Sonya said, handing Jimmy the other cup of hot chocolate in her hand. He took it and went back to standing and talking with Bryson. A few other children their age had gathered, and Sonya grinned. "They're like brothers, those two. They always do everything together."

Sonya continued to tell Caroline how she'd invited Sam to join her for the tree lighting. "When he said you'd be leaving soon and wanted to spend time with you before you left, I understood. Who doesn't want to spend time with a friend before they don't see them for a while?"

Caroline smiled and nodded as Sonya spoke. She glanced back over her shoulder to where Sam had disappeared earlier into the diner. She spotted him outside, standing in the lamplight and talking with an older man. His head was bent, listening intently to the man's words. Yet, something struck inside her, causing her to shiver and Duke to whine. "Sam said he wanted to spend time with me?"

"Looks like the boys are migrating to the other side of the gazebo. We should follow," Sonya said, suddenly. "I don't like to let Jimmy out of my sight. I'm sure Sam would appreciate us keeping an eye on Bryson, too."

Caroline agreed, and she and Sonya walked to the other side of the gazebo, the boys, and the diner, still in sight. Caroline glanced over to Sam on the other side of the street. Her hand tingled with the loss of his holding onto it. From the moment he'd picked her up at Aunt Marge's, their hands hadn't separated.

"I guess you'll be headed back after Christmas," Sonya said.

"Why would you think that?" Caroline watched as Bryson picked up a pile of snow in his hand and tried to form it into a ball. Jimmy did the same with less success. Caroline wanted to go over and show them how to do it right. This wasn't the kind of snow good for snowball fights or snowmen, which seemed to be the children's intent.

"Sam said you had a job in Louisville. That's far, but then, you always wanted to go on an adventure, right?" Sonya sipped her hot chocolate. "We all thought with the floral shop open again, you'd be staying. The way your sister talks, it is as if you'd come home for good. I'm sorry about the divorce. I — I know what losing a husband is like, only different."

Caroline nodded slowly, thinking about what it would be like to leave this place, leave Aunt Marge, her family, Bryson, and most of all... Sam. Maybe when she first came here, that had been her goal. What right did Sam have to share that with Sonya? How many others would know by the end of the night?

"It just wasn't meant to be," Caroline said.

Caroline watched as Sam headed across the street. He stopped and spoke with another man, juggling three drinks in his arms.

"Do you know who will run the shop after you leave? Has Marge changed her mind about closing up the shop and the B&B?"

Startled at the question, Caroline shook her head. "I should help Sam with those drinks before he spills them." And anything else she told him, he seemed to think was okay to tell other people. Why did she think she could trust him?

What did it matter?

"He's such a great guy," Sonya sighed, looking at him. "He'd do anything to help a friend. It's a shame you're leaving." But it didn't sound like it by the tone of her voice. "Maybe when you're in town again, you can come and visit us. We can catch up on life and what's happening in the city."

Caroline didn't answer, but she smiled and tugged on Duke's leash to signal they were about to walk again. "Let's go on home. It's getting late, and we still have to get up in the morning for the craft bazaar." Not to mention she felt like a popsicle. Duke walked stiffly beside her as she went to meet Sam.

"Here, you look cold." He handed her the hot chocolate. A little wisp of steam rose from the hole in the lid for sipping.

"Bryson is with Jimmy. I hope you don't mind. Sonya is keeping watch over them. They might be building a snowman."

"Sounds fun. Should we help?" He gave her a white-toothed grin.

Caroline glanced over her shoulder. Jimmy ran toward his mother, tugging on her scarf until she relented and allowed him to pull it free. He raced off again as the others worked on constructing the snowman.

"I think it's time for Duke and me to go home." Duke agreed, tugging on her leash to keep them from walking.

"I'll grab Bryson and take you home."

"No," she said, suddenly feeling tired. "Don't take him from the fun."

"I brought you. I'll take you home."

"It's not that far for me and Duke to walk back to Aunt Marge's. We've walked this far before," Caroline said.

"It's dark, and I wouldn't feel right," Sam insisted. "Just wait right here for a minute, and I'll be back to take you." He raced over, had a few words with Sonya, and returned. "Ready?"

"You should be with your son."

"And I will be once I see you home. What kind of friend would I be not to make sure you get home safe?"

Friend. Caroline pressed her lips together. She and Duke went with Sam. They got in his truck, him turning up the heat as soon as the air in the vent wouldn't blast them with arctic winds. Back at Aunt Marge's Sam parked and rushed to get her door. First, he let Duke out, who sat like a good boy in the truck's back seat.

As Caroline headed for the porch, Sam asked, "Did you have a good time?"

"I did. The carolers surprised me. I haven't heard people singing Christmas songs together in a long while."

"Not even in church?" Sam asked.

"Hymns, but not carols."

"I'm glad you liked them." Sam lingered, shifting weight from one foot to the other.

"What about you?" Caroline asked, wanting to be polite and eager to get inside where she could sort her feelings away from him.

"I like the lights," Sam said, smiling at Caroline. "But I like you better."

Her breath caught, and she couldn't speak.

Sam's face was so close, his hazel eyes wide, his lips pursed, and his bottom lip protruded slightly. Caroline's face flushed, heat creeping up her neck.

The light from the porch lamp fell on his face. She tried to take a deep breath. Deep, smoky coffee and fresh-cut pine drew her closer and made her stomach tighten.

Sam's self-confidence froze her in place. He had been so shy and quiet back when they were younger. "Sam," she whispered, finding her voice hoarse. Hopeful.

Heat radiated off him, caressing her, tempting her to step out of the cold and into his arms. She wanted to stay there forever, pressing against him and letting his warmth seep into her body.

Sam moved his hands to her shoulders, and Caroline felt a wave of pleasure course through her body. His forehead touched hers, his nose sliding down the length of hers. His lips were like paradise against a tundra, melting away all thoughts she could form.

All the fear, doubt, and worry dissolved as her senses filled with Sam's presence. He pulled her closer, their bodies flush against each other, lapping up the warmth radiating from him, created between them. She gasped in surprise when he kissed her more firmly, as if asking for permission to come closer.

His hand had found its way to the back of her neck, pulling her head closer while his other slid over the curve of her waist, exploring farther down until it came to rest on the swell of her hipbone.

She should pull away; this was not right, but she leaned into Sam and surrendered to his kiss. When they finally parted, gasps were exchanged like a secret language between them that needed no words. Intensity still held them together until finally Sam released his hold on Caroline and stepped back, looking at her with something akin to awe in his eyes that left Caroline feeling a little breathless.

"I-I'm sorry," he stammered out before quickly regaining himself. "I shouldn't have done that."

Caroline shook herself out of the trance-like state she found herself in and took another step backward, putting some much-needed space between them. "Why?" she asked softly, hoping that she sounded calmer than she felt inside.

But reality held its ground, and Sam stepped back quickly. "I can't do this. I mean, I want to, but..."

"But what?"

Sam's face softened, his lips parted as if he was going to say something else but thought better of it and turned quickly away instead. "I can't do this again. I'm sorry."

He strode off the porch, leaving her standing there in front of the doorway, the cold settling into her bones. A shiver slipped down her spine.

Sam got into his truck and pull away.

"Carrie, dear. What are you doing out here in the cold?" Aunt Marge stood holding the door, Duke standing behind her.

Caroline stared out at the space where Sam's truck had been parked moments ago before turning to go inside.

"Is everything alright?"

Caroline could never hide her true feelings from Aunt Marge. As soon as the door shut behind her, the elderly woman clucked her tongue. "This calls for tea."

Chapter Nineteen

"Is that Caroline with her sisters? You should invite her to dinner." Sam's mother, Pam, gave him a nudge after church.

"Where?"

His mother lifted a brow. "Don't play that game with me, Samuel Brink."

"I don't know what you're talking about," he grumbled, searching the crowd of people leaving for his son.

"She was at the craft bazaar yesterday. You would have known if you took Bry and went."

"I had to work." He leaned around his mother and waved, spotting Bry with Jimmy. Sonya caught his wave and smiled.

"You're like your father, always working and not taking a moment to look at what's around you."

"What's that supposed to mean?"

His mother sighed and placed a hand on his arm. "I'm grateful you took the morning off, and you're here. I get to spend the day with my boys. Although, I wouldn't mind if you invited a guest," his mother hinted. "And I don't mean Sonya and Jimmy." She looked pointedly across the church foyer, where Sonya and the boys headed toward them.

"I'm sure Carrie's family appreciates getting to spend all the time they can with her." Sam pulled on the ends of the long sleeves of his sweater. It itched around his neck.

"Carrie is it?" His mother looked more amused. Then she dismissed his slip-up of using Caroline's nickname with the wave of her hand. "Poor girl has probably had enough of her mother and sisters. Why don't you go over and rescue her?"

"She looks content where she is." His mind went back to the porch and the way she molded in his arms. "Her sisters will be upset if I go interfering."

"Didn't you tell me Janelle asked you to spend time with her?"

"I did."

His mother stepped around, blocking his view of the hall, and Sonya. "Sam." She used that scolding voice when he was about to get a lecture.

"I'm a grown man. I don't need my mother trying to set me up." His eyes stayed on Bry, talking and hanging out with Jimmy. Bry's red jacket was tied around his waist, and he had his Sunday School papers in hand.

"I didn't realize I was. Since you've been spending so much time there and Bry talks about her so much, I thought you'd like to have her over instead of going there for once."

Sam shook his head. "She'll be leaving soon. There's no sense in getting your hopes up." He looked at his mother, her skeptical look twisting at his insides.

"What makes you think she's leaving?"

"She told me." He tried to step around his mother, but she kept him blocked.

Her chin tilted in challenge. "She's got the flower shop open again."

"Only because Marge asked her to open it over the holidays."

"I heard she remodeled it. You made the shelves, didn't you? Sounds like a lot for a few weeks."

He hated it when his mother did this to him. Put him in this position. In public. At church, no less. "Marge wanted to open it back up."

"Is that right?"

Sam ran a hand down over his chin. He reached out a hand about to call for Bry when his mother clasped his hand. "You never could lie well."

"Lie?" Sam scowled. Sonya and the boys had stopped to talk with another woman and her daughter a few feet away.

"She's not Megan."

"I know. Now, I need to get Bry, and we should get home." Every second he waited to go fetch Bry, sweat beaded on his brow.

His mother refused to budge. "Marge didn't want to open that shop up again. We all know she's closing things down and slowing down to retire. The shop is all Caroline's."

"Then it's only open for the holidays." Sam couldn't stress enough. He no longer wanted to talk about it. Reaching up, he couldn't ignore the itching of the dark wool against his skin.

"I heard she was going to do the flowers for the Lehman and Evans wedding next month. That's after the holidays."

He supposed if they were silk flowers, she could create them and fill the order. He took a step toward Bry, not wanting to take this conversation any further. Especially here. His mother stepped in front of him. "Sam." She looked him in the eye. "I know you like her. I've always known you liked her."

"Mom." He groaned inside.

"Don't think I didn't notice you looking over at her while Pastor Lawrence gave his sermon."

Of course, his mother would notice. The entire time, Sam sat in the pew staring straight ahead, trying not to see how the light of the morning sun streaked through the stained-glass windows, dappling on her. Light shone in her hair, making the waves of her brown mane glow with the sun's warmth, glistening like strands of cinnamon. The red dress was more conservative than the others, but it still glowed with a merriment of its own. The dress hugged her body, the soft material shimmering with the light, highlighting her curves, hiding nothing. It should have been illegal to wear a dress like that to church, thought Sam.

"Go. Ask her to dinner. Take her out if not bring her back to the house. I'll get Bry and meet you at the car."

"No."

Sonya and the boys headed toward him.

Yet, he couldn't make his feet move to go in search of Caroline.

"I never took my son as a coward." His mother glanced at him with such sympathy in her eyes it made Sam retreat within himself. He swore he wouldn't ever allow another woman to hold this kind of control over him. Caroline made him think about futures and families, which he hadn't thought of in a long time. But now wasn't the time to ponder this.

"There you are," his mother said, as Sonya and the boys approached. "Are you ready Bry?"

"Can I go with Jimmy?" Bry asked.

"Tanner dropped off our tree yesterday. Jimmy and I were going to make popcorn and decorate the tree. You're welcome to join us." Sonya wore a white cable-knit sweater dress and navy leggings with her tan fuzzy boots.

Shaking out of his trance, Sam swallowed hard. Nodded. He avoided his mother's gaze.

"Yes!" Bry did an air punch.

"Can I ride with Jimmy?" Bry asked.

"Sure," Sam said, "I'll see you there."

Sonya gathered the boys and hurried through the lingering crowd to leave.

He held up his hand, feeling his mother's silent words pressing to come out. "I'll take you home."

Escorting his mother out of the church, Sam looked through the people exiting for any sign of Caroline or that alluring red dress. Not seeing her anywhere, he excused himself and went in the opposite direction, needing to gather their coats. He heard laughter coming from down the opposite hall. As he got closer, he could make out the voices of two women happily chatting about something that sounded like flowers—which meant it must be Caroline and Marge!

Hadn't he seen her earlier with her sisters?

He stopped when he reached the coat closet. "Caroline..." he whispered as he stepped into view. She spun around in surprise before finally settling into a smile when she saw who it was. "Morning, Sam," she acknowledged him before turning back to Marge with an apologetic smile on her face. "Should we go?"

Marge just chuckled, as if this happened all the time, before nodding toward Sam with a knowing smile on her face. Her gray hair was as gray as the clouds in winter, though her face was never wrinkled, and her eyes were as bright as stars. The woman didn't look a day over sixty. "I'm sure you'll catch up."

"I missed you yesterday," Caroline said, tugging on her black wool jacket.

Sam spotted his jacket and reached for it and his mother's. "Mom's waiting. Bry went with Sonya." He didn't know why he felt the need to explain. It wasn't as if he owed her any explanation.

"Will you be at the Christmas Eve party Rob and Kelly are throwing?"

"Hard to say." He watched as her face fell. "I got to go."

"Of course." She followed him out of the closet. "Sam, about last night—"

"It shouldn't have happened." He never meant to hurt her. "I said I was sorry."

"I know, but I can't help wondering why?"

"Why?" He took another step back.

"I thought we were friends?"

"Friends don't kiss friends, Caroline. I got to go." Sam spun on his heel and stalked down the hall in a hurry to get away. Tension coiled deeper in his belly until the cold air of the outside hit his lungs and forced him to relax. *Why?* echoed in his head. It wasn't fair. Life wasn't fair. God knew he couldn't handle having another woman he loved walking out of his life again. He should have known better than to think he could be around Caroline and not fall in love.

Chapter Twenty

Caroline forgot how bossy her sister could be. Janelle insisted they all show up at her parents' house by eleven o'clock to open presents. She liked to organize and plan everything. She always had.

The house smelled of honey ham and pineapple upside-down cake. Baked beans cooked in the oven and fresh buns waited to get warmed before they ate. Brenda wore a green velvet dress with ruffles around the bottom. She'd left her hair down for once.

Janelle fussed over the kids while carefully ensuring nothing got on her festive red sweater. She kept her hair pulled back to show off the diamonds on her ears. Every once in a while, she'd give Caroline a long, uncomfortable look. Caroline headed to the kitchen to offer to help her mom but got shooed out of the way. Instead of going back into the living room, she slipped on her boots and went outside. Halfway to the barn, Janelle called after, "Don't you dare go out there and bring the stink back inside."

Caroline glanced over her shoulder. "Then I suppose I can go back to Aunt Mar's. I don't think anyone will miss me. By the looks you've been giving me, I'd guess you'd be happy not to have me come back inside."

She knew she shouldn't fight with Janelle. Not on Christmas. Forgive her Lord, she didn't feel like celebrating anyone's birthday. Ever since Sam kissed her and then avoided her, the weight of his rejection seemed to put a heavier burden on her.

"And how am I looking at you, Caroline?" Janelle stomped closer, arms crossed. It warmed a few degrees in the passing days, but not enough for one to go without a coat. "What do you think Mom and Dad are going to do when they find out you're leaving? Do you have any idea how much you hurt them the first time?"

"Hurt them? I went to college, Janelle. Josh proposed. I got married. Now, I'm home."

Janelle narrowed her eyes. "We told you not to marry Josh. He only wanted you to work while he went to school. He had no intentions of ever providing for you, Caroline, or having a family. We all knew that. We tried to tell you, and you wouldn't listen then and you are not listening now."

"It's Christmas." Caroline should have figured things were going too well with her family for it to last long. "I don't know why you're dragging out the past. Josh isn't my husband anymore, and I don't work to keep him going to school for free anymore either."

"But you're going back. Got yourself a new position after Aunt Mar gave you the flower shop. You know I offered to buy it, move there, and run the B&B, but she wouldn't sell it. Couldn't figure out why. Then when we knew you were coming back, I talked her into opening the floral shop. I know how much you loved that place. I can't let you hurt Mom and Dad again."

Janelle gave Aunt Mar the idea for her to run the shop? Janelle couldn't have made Aunt Mar ill, but the shop hadn't needed to reopen.

"What nonsense!" Aunt Marge's voice rang out. She held Aunt Maeve by the hand, helping her along the shoveled path. "Help Maeve inside before you cause any more trouble."

Janelle glowered at Aunt Mar, then looked back at Caroline.

"I know you're leaving. You do and don't think you'll be welcome to come back again." She sniffed.

"Who said anything about Caroline leaving?" Aunt Mar asked, holding onto Maeve, who took small steps because of her arthritis. It must have gotten worse with the change in the weather. Caroline headed toward them to help her aunt.

"Carrie's leaving?" Maeve asked.

"I was, but don't you worry, Aunt Maeve. I am not going any farther than Aunt Mar's place."

"To pack." Janelle shivered despite her best effort. She bit her lip after the bitter words came out.

"Maybe to box up the Lehman and Evan's wedding bouquets I've been working on," Caroline took Aunt Maeve's other side to help her. "Where's your walker?" she asked.

"Don't need no walker." Aunt Maeve snorted. "I'm as young and spry as you." She winked.

Caroline admired Aunt Maeve's spunk, the oldest of the three sisters.

"I know you're lying," Janelle confronted them. "Sonya told me that Sam told her about your new job and you leaving. Why, I'm surprised you are still here."

Janelle never was good at holding things in for long. They festered and spilled over. Caroline glanced at Aunt Mar over Aunt Maeve's scarfed head. In her aging years, Aunt Maeve had hunched over, more so after their father passed, and she had no one to care for anymore.

"Maybe because she isn't going anywhere." Aunt Mar clucked her tongue. "You should know better than to listen to gossip, Janelle Marian Adams. Does your husband know you're out here harassing your sister over hearsay?" Aunt Marge let go of Aunt Maeve for a moment.

"Terrible child," grumbled Aunt Maeve. "Always wanted to stir trouble, that one. You be careful." She looked at Caroline. "You help me inside before my bones freeze."

"Absolutely." Caroline glanced over her shoulder at the barn.

She figured her father went to check on the cows before they all sat down to dinner. She'd have to wait for another time to go out and help him. Before she moved away from home, the second place beyond Aunt Mar and the floral shop she found refuge in was the barn with her father.

"It's not causing trouble. It's true. Sonya wouldn't lie to me."

"Not intentionally, I'm sure," Aunt Marge agreed.

"Are you calling Sam a liar?"

Caroline stamped her foot, having enough of this. "Stop, Janelle. That's enough."

"Yes. Enough." Aunt Maeve's false teeth chattered. Caroline leaned into her to offer some warmth. The purple winter coat with black velvet around the neck and fur around the hood should have been enough to keep her frail aunt comfortable. No wonder Aunt Marge spoke many times about going to stay with Maeve. Caroline's heart sank. How long would she have before her aunt sought heaven?

This was why she knew she couldn't leave. Sam or no Sam, she loved her family. Even Janelle standing there being... Well... being Janelle.

The door opened, and Ben, Janelle's husband, peered out the door. "Janelle, your mom's looking for you to help set the table."

Maeve waved. "Now there's a big, strong man to get me in out of the cold."

Ben chuckled. He ducked back inside and a moment later, came out with boots on. "To the rescue, Aunt Maeve."

Caroline released her hold.

Ben looked at Janelle. He whispered something to her, and her face became grim. "I mean it, Janelle. It's Christmas. Let it be."

Once Maeve was in the house, snug as a bug, Caroline grabbed some hot tea and stepped into the mudroom to collect herself.

Brenda brought Janelle, causing Caroline to stiffen.

"Apologize, now!" Brenda said.

Caroline's mouth slackened. Apologize?

Then she realized Brenda had spoken to Janelle.

"I won't," Janelle hissed. "I have nothing to apologize for."

"How about helping to spread lies?" Brenda glared at Janelle, who gasped.

"Girls?" Dorothy called. "We're about to start dinner."

"You two best make up. I'm not sitting through dinner with this hanging in the air, not on Christmas. It's not fair to the rest of us."

"Fair?" Caroline put her tea down on the wooden bench her father used to put his boots on and take them off. "What's not fair is being accused of things without asking. What's not fair is having my older sister try to control my life and interfere because she thinks she knows everything and her decisions are the best." Once Caroline got going, she couldn't stop.

"It would be nice for once to have a loving, supportive family that doesn't throw things in your face when they go wrong. I don't need reminding that my marriage ended or that I don't have children like you, Janelle. Nor do I need you to find me friends or try to get me a job to make me stay. I came home, and yes, I got offered a job. And yes, I told Sam, and I told him I was considering it. He had no right to tell others, but if you must know I turned down that job because it was pointless to go back to a place where I had nothing and no one left of importance in my life except for the few people in my Bible Study. They encouraged me to come home. Here I am. Sorry about your luck, Janelle, but the only place I'm going is home... to Aunt Marge's. And you can tell Sonya she's got nothing to worry about because Sam isn't interested in me, not like that. We're just friends." Caroline grabbed her coat. She hadn't taken off her boots and headed for the door.

"Carrie." Her mother stood in the doorway as she left.

Outside, she nearly forgot about Duke. Her parents wouldn't let him in the house, so she needed to go to the barn, anyway.

Headed inside, she heard a hammer and her father's voice. Duke barked, and she was never happier to see him.

"That should do it, Paul,"

Caroline froze at the sound of Sam's voice. What was he doing here? In her father's barn. On Christmas.

Chapter Twenty-One

"I appreciate you coming over and giving me a hand. I'd have had a bigger problem later. The girls don't come close to the barn anymore." Paul chuckled. "They're afraid I'll put them to work," Paul said.

"Hey!" Caroline stood, her fancy wool jacket on, Duke at her side. "I would have helped if you'd told me you needed help. You shouldn't have bothered Sam and taken him from his family."

"Didn't want you messing up those fancy clothes before dinner." Paul picked up the last of the tools. "Besides, I figured you'd been in the city for so long you'd turned into your sisters and would avoid this place."

"Why does everyone keep making assumptions about me?" Caroline scowled. Sam couldn't seem to find words, too enamored by the way she looked, standing there inside the barn's milk house. Behind him was the milk tank they'd fixed. It hummed lazily, the cooling unit working once more.

"I know my girls," Paul said. "I suspect you came out here to get me for dinner. Well, thank you again, Sam. I'll see you get paid a little extra for coming on a holiday."

"Think nothing of it," Sam managed. He grabbed the rest of his tools and shoved them in his tool bag.

"Don't take too long," Paul said to the two of them. "Your mother will want to eat while it's hot."

"More like she's burning the buns and Dad is in a hurry to get inside before all the good ones are gone," Caroline said after her father's departure.

Realizing he'd been left alone with Caroline, Sam hurried to grab the last pair of pliers. Duke sat, tail thumping on the cement floor. "I'm surprised he's not in the house."

"Dad doesn't allow animals in the house," Caroline said.

"At least the milk house is kept warmer than the rest of the barn." Sam wasn't sure what compelled him to keep talking. "It's a good thing he noticed the compressor died this morning, otherwise the milk would have gone bad."

"You're a man of many talents." She reached for Duke's collar and snapped on the leash. "Come, Duke. It's time to go." She hesitated. The look in her eyes could tear a man in two. "Merry Christmas, Sam."

Suddenly panicked at her departure, Sam asked, "I thought Duke couldn't go inside."

Caroline glanced over her shoulder at him, and his inside melted clean to his toes. Those eyes sent a heart-wrenching reality through him. What if this was his last chance to see her again?

Caroline reached for the door.

"Wait. Caroline. Don't go."

"Oh, and you can tell Bryson there's something for him at Aunt Marge's for the next time he comes over." But she didn't sound happy about it. And he could only blame himself.

She turned the knob and let the cold air inside. He grabbed his jacket, having taken it off earlier. The flannel he wore was too thin against the winter weather. "Hold on, Carrie."

That seemed to hold her. She watched as he slipped on his jacket.

"Don't call me that," she said. "You've got no right. Not after all the trouble you've caused." Then she turned, the door closing them back in again. Duke standing between them. A slight growl came from him as if he sensed his owner's displeasure.

"I get you're upset with me for not talking to you for this past week, but I can explain. I want to explain. Please. If you'll let me," he blabbered on, hoping if he kept talking she would keep staying there with him.

"While I don't appreciate you ghosting me, I also don't appreciate you sharing my business with Sonya and having her tell Janelle who now thinks I'm leaving!! Have you any idea what you've done?"

No. He didn't. Sam shook his head.

"Janelle threatened to never talk to me again if I hurt my parents by leaving and going back to Louisville."

"And that's a bad thing?" Sam asked.

Her lips twitched for a moment, then they went right back to their deep frown. "Yes. My family thinks I'm leaving because of you!"

Sam put down the toolbox, feeling unbalanced. "You are leaving. Aren't you? Didn't you say you had this new job and had to go soon?"

Caroline's expression made him feel an even bigger heel. "Carrie?"

Those tear-rimmed eyes, flushed red cheeks, and flaring nostrils told him she was more upset with him than sad. What had he done? Dawning lit on him. "I'm sorry. About Sonya. I meant nothing. You said you were leaving."

"No, Sam." Caroline gripped Duke's leash. "You said I was leaving. Did it ever occur to you to ask before assuming?"

Oh, shoot. He'd screwed up. Big Time. The pressure in his chest eased slightly. Caroline was staying. "You didn't take the job?"

She shook her head.

"You're staying?"

"I'm here, aren't I?"

"Um." Sam cupped the back of his neck. His ears burned with embarrassment. "Yeah."

"I'll see you around, Sam."

"See you around." Wait. What was he doing? Caroline and Duke stepped outside the milk house. He watched out the window of the door, but she didn't head back inside the house. Hadn't her father said they were about to sit down to eat? He checked his watch. He needed to get home to Bryson. His mother expected to have Christmas dinner later that night. If Caroline wasn't going in the house for dinner, then he would invite her to his. Sam stalked off, determined to catch up, but Caroline pulled out of the lane, and he ran to his truck to catch up.

Lord, don't let me screw this up a second time.

He followed her the entire way from her parents' house to Marge's big old Victorian house on Main Street. By the time she made it to the porch, Sam was at the steps. "Caroline Adams, I love you."

Caroline opened the door and let Duke go ahead of her inside. She stood staring at him, the door ajar. He strolled up to her. "Aren't you going to invite me inside?"

She blinked. The shock of his words made her go pale. A coil in his gut twisted. Would she run? He pressed his hand against her back. "It'll be warmer if we go in."

She nodded, stepping in and holding the door. After he stepped inside, she closed the door. Turning away, she shed her jacket and put it on a chair. Duke went into another room, most likely to find his bed or the couch. He wondered if Caroline even tried to push the pooch off after Bryson allowed the dog to lie beside him and watch television all the time.

The picture of Bryson here with Caroline and him wouldn't leave his thoughts. She walked into the living room, where the tall pine he delivered stood decked out with lights and big glass bulbs. An angel stared down at them from the top of the tree. She kneeled down, pulled out a package, and handed it up to him. "This is for Bryson."

Lowering to his knees in front of her, Sam placed his hands over hers. "Caroline. Did you hear what I said?"

Her gaze fell to the brown packaging, and the plaid ribbon tied around it. "Make sure you tell him it's from Aunt Mar and Duke and me."

"And what about me?" Sam's voice turned husky. He rubbed his thumb against the inside of her cool wrist. "A man says he loves you, and you keep him hanging."

Her gaze met his. For once in his life, he found the courage to brave the future. A peace settled inside him. "Say something. Anything."

"No."

That one word had shattered his life before. His hands tightened their hold on hers. "What do you mean, no?"

"No." She yanked her hands from him and put down the gift on his lap. "You don't get to tell me you love me, Samuel Brink. You're not allowed to do that."

"Why?"

"Because.... Because... We're friends."

"Shouldn't friends love one another?" Sam asked.

"You ghosted me." She looked so cute, with her arms and legs crossed, glowering at him.

"I did. Let me explain."

One eyebrow rose in response.

"I was afraid you were going to leave. You need to understand. Bryson's mother, Megan. She said no, Carrie. Not just no to me, but no to him. I offered to make her my wife. I loved her and she left us. She walked out on us. I wasn't ready to go through that again. Bryson doesn't remember Megan. I don't even have a picture out. Someday if he asks, I'll show him, but she chooses not to be in his life. I didn't want you to leave. I didn't want to feel this way, but I do, and I'm not taking no for an answer this time."

Her arms slackened, and she wrung her hands together. "I loved Josh, too. And he used me. He wanted a lifelong career of being a student, and I wanted a family. I made a big mistake, and it cost me so much. I look at you and Bryson and I—"

"We love you, Caroline. Bryson loves you. He asked you to be his mother!"

"And that upset you," she whispered.

"It did, but only because I had feelings for you then. Tell me, Caroline, you feel it, too."

She chewed on her lip for several moments. The phone rang somewhere from within her coat pockets. Her family realized most likely she wasn't coming in for dinner.

"I do, but you said you wanted to be friends. And Sonya..."

"Forget Sonya. She's got good intentions and bad delivery." Sam slid closer. "We have this special relationship because we're single parents, but it's nothing more than a friendship. Nothing like what I feel for you," Sam said.

Tears swam in Caroline's eyes. "I'm sorry,"

"You have nothing to apologize for. I am the one who screwed this up. The one who kissed you and ran away. I'm sorry. Please, Caroline. Let me make it up to you. My mother wanted me to invite you to dinner. Come have Christmas dinner with us. I want you to become a part of our family."

Caroline sucked in a breath.

"All I'm asking for is dinner, and maybe a date after that, and another date, and another, until one day we both decide we're ready for more."

Tears spilled over her lashes. Quickly, she nodded.

He yanked her into his arms. She laughed, and he joined her. In the background, the phone rang again. "Should you answer that? It's probably your mother or Janelle."

"They can wait." Caroline wrapped her arms around his neck. "I've got something more important to do."

"And what is that?" Sam bent his head, hoping.

She grinned. "Kissing the man I love."

Duke poked his head out over the arm of the couch, but Sam wasn't about to spoil the moment by telling on the dog. He wrapped his arms tighter around Caroline, pulling her closer and finding her lips. She tasted like everything he remembered and more. She tasted like home, with a hint of spice and something sweet. Having her in his embrace never felt more right. A tiny sound escaped her, something more than a sigh. He understood it and echoed it as he deepened the kiss. He gave in to the moment, allowing the warmth to spread between them until he knew if he continued to kiss her this way, he'd have to propose, and she'd think him crazy. Unable to bear hearing her say "'no," he pulled back and nuzzled his face in her neck for a moment while he gained his thoughts again. How would he ever think again, intoxicated by the feel of her in his arms? Safe. Home.

Epilogue

ONE YEAR LATER

"Oh, aren't these the cutest?" Bridget held up the plaid heart ornament. "These holiday hearts were the best idea!" She beamed at Caroline. "You'll have to show me how you made them."

Caroline added a few more to the tree inside the living room, at the bed-and-breakfast. Aunt Mar and Aunt Maeve sat on the loveseat while many of their friends joined in trimming the tree. Caroline glanced over at Sam, who flashed her a grin while he talked with Luke, Rob, and Tanner. The other Evans brother stood in the kitchen with his daughter and once-again pregnant wife to sample the cookies made by Dani at the new bakery. Brenda made the logo for the shop, as she now did for most of the places in town. Janelle used an excuse of having a party to attend for the bank, and while Caroline and her sister were civil, she appreciated not having the extra drama. Everyone brought an ornament to put on their tree, a tradition they hoped to continue each Christmas running the B & B. So far, the holiday hearts were Caroline's favorite. She'd made them with an old flannel shirt of Sam's and a lot of love.

Rob clasped Sam on the back as he passed through the room. Shouts of joy lifted, and Caroline couldn't feel more happy and at home. Bryson and a few other children played in the parlor, with Duke keeping an eye on them. Marah Lehman approached her, thanking her for a third time for including her mother Penny in the celebration. Penny sat in the rocker near the French doors, watching everyone milling around. She wore a bright pink velvet dress, which helped Marah spot her in the crowd.

Caroline's own mother fussed in the kitchen, pretending like the party had been her idea, but Caroline didn't mind. It kept her mother busy.

Sam snuck up behind her and wrapped his arm around her. "I think this is the perfect time, don't you?" he whispered in her ear.

Caroline leaned back and held out her hand where a silver band glinted on her finger. She'd been waiting all evening for a time like this. Reaching around, Sam twisted the ring, allowing the small cluster of diamonds to sparkle. As if it turned on a switch, Bridget, Brenda, Ann, and Marah came to admire it.

"Everyone," Sam boomed, "Caroline and I have an announcement to make!"

"They're engaged!" Brenda burst out, and poor Sam's face fell. Caroline turned from the ladies, taking his face into her hands. "As if you didn't think they wouldn't know." She smiled, loving this man more and more each day. She drew his face closer and gave him a small peck on the cheek. One was never enough with Sam. The next one she went to plant on him landed on his lips.

"Hey. None of that until the wedding!" someone called out.

Caroline sprang back, her face turning a little hot. Sam tucked her in against her side. "You should tell them the date."

"Yes," Bridge said. "When is the blessed event?"

Caroline glanced around the room, her heart swelling. Sam's parents had arrived late because of his mother's schedule. His mother assured them they wouldn't miss it for the world.

"Maybe this time," Caroline said to her sister, "we should let Sam make the announcement."

Brenda shrugged.

"You're all invited," Sam said, everyone in the room gone quiet with anticipation. He glanced over at Caroline, her stomach doing a little flip.

"When is it?" Rob called from the other end of the room, sitting with his wife on his lap.

"Tell them." Caroline nudged him, the anticipation getting to her.

"Tonight," Sam said.

Everyone in the room glanced around.

"Caroline and I decided what better place for us to say our vows than in a room full of people whom we love? So right here, right now, in front of this beautiful tree, and with all of you and God as our witness, we're going to get married."

Murmurs went around the room, then suddenly everyone was happily chattering, and Caroline's mother came and shoved her toward the door. "I guess that's my cue to get changed."

She'd bought a simple white gown for the occasion.

"I see your father." Sam kissed her on the forehead.

"Which means Pastor Lawrence is here," she finished for him.

As her mother pushed her toward the stairs, she heard a door and, as she glanced back, spotted Janelle coming in with Ben, and their boys followed behind them. By the look on her sister's face, she was none too happy about leaving her bank Christmas party, but Caroline's husband grinned. Their father must have told him what was going on. So much for the surprise. Caroline climbed the stairs, taking a moment to look back one final time before becoming Mrs. Samuel Brink.

Bonus Content

Want more? I've got some bonus content for you! Sign up for my mailing list. You'll receive access to special bonus content for some of my books, exclusive for my subscribers. Signing up will let you hear about my next release as soon as it is out. And.... you get a free book!

As always... Thanks for reading my books and enjoy the romance.

Get A Free Book!

Join my mailing list to be the first to know of new releases, free books, special prices and other great stuff.

www.readslower.com

About the Author

Growing up on a farm in Pennsylvania, Susan Lower yearned for adventure. A woodsy gal, Susan prefers camping over going to the beach any day. Still a farm girl at heart, Susan writes fast action reads filled with cowboys, heroes, and hope. She writes both western historical and contemporary romances, romantic suspense, and has been itching to one day write a mystery or thriller. Christmas is her favorite holiday, and she loves to write resilient characters struggling to overcome the complications of life while holding their values and strengthening their faith.

Also by Susan Lower

Silver Wind Horse Rescue
Forgotten Reins

Unbridled

Silver Stirrups

Hearts of Hidden Hills
Salvaged Hearts

Reckless Hearts

Healing Hearts

Holiday Hearts

Thunder Valley MC
Haden

Rosco

Cowgirl Mysteries
The Cowgirl Gets The Bad Guy

The Cowgirl Takes The Bounty

The Cowgirl Chases The Robbers

Brides of Annie's Creek Novella Series
The Fruitcake Bride

The Thimble Bride

The Postage Stamp Bride

Made in United States
Cleveland, OH
22 January 2026